"Right. So [barcode obscured] **on my flight t** [barcode obscured] **in L.A. The cl** [barcode obscured] **be a problem.** [obscured] **coming."** He started out the door, then stopped in the hallway. **"I just thought…can you get someone to cover while we're gone?"**

Cover the office, he meant. They were never both gone at the same time. Or they never had been before. Except once. In Vegas four years ago.

Sadie met his gaze. "I can get someone. Don't worry. Thank you for seeing me here. I won't keep you."

"Good." There was another pause. He shifted awkwardly. "Thanks." Then he cleared his throat. "I meant what I said earlier, Sadie. You don't have to quit."

That was what all this hemming and hawing was about? He was stalling until he found a way to work that into the conversation.

"It can be like before. We can just go back to—"

"Goodnight, Spence," she said abruptly.

And she shut the door in his face.

Chosen by him for business,
taken by him for pleasure…

A classic collection of office romances
from Modern™ Romance by your favourite authors

Look out for more, coming soon!

THE BOSS'S WIFE
FOR A WEEK

BY
ANNE McALLISTER

MILLS & BOON

Pure reading pleasure

All the characters in this book have no existence outside the imagination
of the author, and have no relation whatsoever to anyone bearing the
same name or names. They are not even distantly inspired by any
individual known or unknown to the author, and all the incidents are
pure invention.

First published in Great Britain 2007
Harlequin Mills & Boon Limited,
Eton House, 18-24 Paradise Road, Richmond, Surrey TW9 1SR

© Barbara Schenck 2007

ISBN-13: 978 0 263 85353 7

Set in Times Roman 10¼ on 12 pt
01-0907-52476

Printed and bound in Spain
by Litografia Rosés, S.A., Barcelona

Award-winning author **Anne McAllister** was once given a blueprint for happiness that included a nice, literate husband, a ramshackle Victorian house, a horde of mischievous children, a bunch of big friendly dogs, and a life spent writing stories about tall, dark and handsome heroes. 'Where do I sign up?' she asked, and promptly did. Lots of years later, she's happy to report the blueprint was a success. She's always happy to share the latest news with readers at her website: www.annemcallister.com, and welcomes their letters there or at P.O. Box 3904, Bozeman, Montana 59772, USA (SASE appreciated).

For Haine, in friendship forever,
and for Chuck who taught Ted everything he knew.
So it's the wrong book. We know life isn't fair,
but thanks for making mine so much better

CHAPTER ONE

IT WAS paperwork that kept Sadie Morrissey tied to Spencer Tyack. He was hopeless at it.

If paperwork were left to Spence it would never get done. And that was no way to run a business. Tyack Enterprises was an enormously successful property development business because Spence had a good eye, great insight and a prodigious work ethic—and because he had Sadie to take care of the details.

She'd been doing it for years, ever since she'd been in high school and he'd been barely twenty-one, a boy from the wrong side of the tracks with grit and goals and not much else. Now, twelve years later, he owned a multinational business and had his finger in property developments on five continents.

He'd have taken over the world by now, Sadie sometimes thought, except she couldn't keep up with the paperwork.

"You need to file faster," Spence always told her, flashing that megawatt drop-dead gorgeous grin of his as he breezed through the office on his way to London or Paris or Athens or New York.

"Not on your life," Sadie always replied, wadding up a piece of paper and throwing it at him. The grin flashed again and he winked at her.

Sadie resisted the grin, resisted the wink. Resisted Spence— something else she always did.

"I'm busy enough, thank you very much," she told him tartly. "And it's not only filing."

Of course he knew that. He knew it was Sadie who kept things organized, who could lay her hand on any piece of paper at any given moment, who could set up a meeting between people on four continents at the drop of a hat, whose address book was even more stuffed full of information than his own.

He only said it to annoy her. Then he'd grin again, rattle off half a dozen more things she needed to do, and then he'd vanish, off to catch another plane while Sadie got back to work.

Not that she cared.

Until last year she'd had a reason to stay in Butte. She'd been determined to care for her elderly grandmother, to make sure Gran would be able to stay in her own home as long as possible.

Now that Gran had been gone six months, her parents were urging her to come to Oregon where they lived, and her brother, Danny, had promised her job interviews galore if she came to Seattle.

But Sadie hadn't gone. She liked Butte with its wild and woolly history. Loved Montana. Delighted in the change of seasons, in the wide-open spaces. It was still, as far as she was concerned, the best place on earth.

And she liked her life—what there was of it. Mostly there was her job. But that was all right. She and Spence had always worked well together, and the job was exciting and demanding, even though she was always going like mad, working insane hours as she did her best to keep the ducks in a row and the details aligned so that Spence could get on with buying up the world piece by piece.

Some days—like today—Sadie thought she ought to have been born an octopus. But even eight arms would not have been enough to deal with all the Tyack Enterprises projects she was juggling this afternoon.

The phone had been ringing when she'd opened the office door at eight-thirty this morning. By lunchtime she had talked four times to an Italian determined to encourage Spence's interest in some condominiums in Naples even though she'd assured him that Spence wasn't there, he was in New York. She'd listened to an imperious Greek tycoon named Achilles who wouldn't take no for an answer, either. And in between those and all the other calls, she'd worked on finalizing Spence's meeting in Fiji next week.

Arranging the logistics for him and his co-investors to spend a week on one of Fiji's smaller islands at a resort for stressed-out and overworked businessmen and women was, to put it bluntly, a challenge. Movers and shakers like Spence and his partners did not have schedules that permitted them to laze around for a week in paradise.

"We don't want to laze around," Spence had told her last time he was in Butte. "We just want to go, see the place, crunch the numbers and, if it works out, buy in."

"That's what *you* want," Sadie had agreed. "But Mr. Isogawa wants you to experience the peace you're going to be investing in."

That had been clear during the first conversation she'd had with Japanese businessman Tadahiro Isogawa. Mr. Isogawa wanted partners, yes. But not just any partners. He wanted partners who believed in the resort's concept—and who would experience it firsthand.

"The piece we're investing in?" Spence had frowned. "We don't want a piece. We want partnership in the whole place."

"*P-e-a-c-e,*" Sadie had spelled patiently. "He expects you to all turn up and spend a week getting to know the place—and each other—and reconnecting with your families."

"I don't have a family."

"So tell that to Mr. Isogawa. He's very big on marriage and family. It's why he works, he told me. But he believes sometimes people who work so hard get their priorities mixed up. Hence the need for Nanumi. It's Fijian for 'remember,'" she'd informed Spence. Mr. Isogawa had told her that when he'd explained his reasons for the resort development.

It hadn't impressed Spence. He had given her that sceptical brows-raised look Sadie knew all too well. She'd just shrugged. "Up to you. But he says if you want in, he wants all of you— and your spouses—there for a week to experience it."

Spence had rolled his eyes. But his desire for the resort won out and finally he'd shrugged. "Fine. Whatever he wants. Set it up."

And so she had.

Besides all the rest of her work, it had taken her days to make sure everyone had a clear schedule for the week to come and then to make all the necessary travel arrangements from the far corners of the world to the island resort. In the process she'd answered thousands of questions from astonished spouses who had rung to be sure the proposed week's holiday in Fiji was actually on the level.

"We never get holidays," Marion Ten Eyck had told her. "John is always working."

Steve Walker's wife, Cathy, had said much the same thing. And Richard Carstairs' wife, Leonie, had rung her every day, saying, "Are you sure? Quite sure? Does Richard know?"

And Sadie had assured her over and over that indeed Richard did. She was beginning to think Mr. Isogawa knew what he was talking about.

And just when she finally got everything sorted and began to go over a contract Spence had faxed her for a development in Georgia he was involved in, the phone rang again.

Sadie closed her eyes and prayed for patience. It actually wasn't eight hands she needed, she thought wearily as she reached for the phone. But eight ears certainly wouldn't hurt.

"Tyack Enterprises," she said and was rewarded by the crackle of a transoceanic connection and a voice whose first language was clearly not English. On the plus side, it wasn't Italian or Greek, either.

"Ah, *Isogawa-san, konnichi wa.* How lovely to hear from you!"

And it really was. Mr. Isogawa was the one person she hadn't talked to. "Everyone arrives on Sunday. I have all the details right here."

She happily relayed the information and smiled at his cheerful approval.

Mr. Isogawa, she had discovered, had had little experience with westerners beyond the ones he saw in films. Since Sadie was more given to hard work than car chases and shooting people to get things done, he thought she was a miracle worker. He took all the information as she relayed it, then said, "You must come, too."

"Thank you. I'd love to," Sadie replied with a smile. Who wouldn't want to spend a week in a South Pacific paradise? "But I have work to do here."

"Even so," Mr. Isogawa said. "You work very hard. You should have a holiday, too. A life."

How did he know she didn't have a life?

"You talk to Spencer," he said. "He will arrange it."

Spence didn't take vacations himself. She knew he wouldn't see any reason for anyone else to, either. Officially she had two weeks a year. She couldn't remember ever taking them.

"Maybe someday," she said to Mr. Isogawa. When hell froze over.

Still, after Mr. Isogawa hung up, she thought about what he said.

Not about going to Fiji. There was no chance of that. But maybe she ought to consider getting away. Moving away. For years she'd assured herself that she thrived on the variety and busyness of her life.

But was it really a life?

Rob McConnell, the man she'd been dating for the past few months, was sure it wasn't. "You never have time for anything but your damn job," he complained over and over. "You're not getting any younger, Sadie."

Usually Rob wasn't quite that blunt, but she knew he was getting irritated at her refusal to want more than a casual relationship. She didn't blame him. He was a genuinely nice man. He wanted to marry and have a family. He'd said as much. And he was right, she wasn't getting any younger. She was twenty-eight. If she was going to get serious, she needed to start.

Sadie wanted to get serious. Truly. But not with Rob.

And that was the problem.

Maybe she should move on. She'd been thinking about it ever since her brother, Danny, had come home from Seattle to visit last week, bringing his wife and their one-year-old twins with him. That had been a shock. Danny had always been as footloose as Spence. Seeing her brother as a devoted family man had jolted her.

It seemed to have given Danny pause for thought, too.

"Who'd have thought I'd settle down before you," he'd said the night before he'd left. He'd been sitting in her living room with a twin in each arm, looking exhausted but content. And then he'd considered her slowly, making her squirm under his gaze as he'd said, "But then, you are settled, aren't you, Sadie?"

"What do you mean?"

His mouth twisted. "You're settled in as Spence's drudge."

"I am not!" Sadie had tossed down the copy of Spence's itinerary she'd been going over, making some last-minute adjustments, and jumped up to prowl around the room. "Don't be absurd."

"It isn't me who's being absurd, Sade. It's all work and no play with you. Always has been as been as long as I can remember."

"I play," Sadie had protested.

"When you work seventeen hours instead of eighteen? Hell, you're as driven as Spence."

"We have goals!" she informed him loftily.

"Spence does," Danny had corrected with an elder brother's ruthlessness. "You're just hanging on."

Sadie had whirled around to glare at him. "What's that supposed to mean?"

Danny met her glare head on. "You know damn well what it means"

"I have a great job!"

"But do you have a life? Come on, Sadie. You're the one who always used to name your kids when we were growing up. You're damn near thirty and you barely even date!"

"I'm twenty-eight, not *damn near thirty!* And Rob—"

"You're not serious about Rob McConnell. If you were you'd have invited him over while Kel and I were here. You didn't. So find someone you are serious about. Get married. Have that family you always wanted." He threw the words at her like a gauntlet, and Sadie couldn't pick it up.

"I'm fine," she'd said stiffly.

"Yeah. Sure you are. You could get a job anywhere. Come out to Seattle. Kel will find you a hundred dates. Believe me, you're wasted on Spence."

"I'm not dating Spence."

"And thank God for that," Danny said. "He's my friend, but he's not exactly marriage material, is he?"

He wasn't telling her anything she didn't know. But she shook her head. "I work for him, that's all," she said.

"So quit."

"I can't."

"Why not? Does Spence own your soul?"

"Oh, for heaven's sake. Of course not!" But her face had burned and Sadie had hoped Danny wouldn't notice.

Fortunately he'd just shaken his head. "Well, it makes a guy wonder. You've been working for him for years! Since high school."

"Because he needed the help. You know Spence. He's great at wheeling and dealing. Great at finding properties and renovating them. Great at potential. He can see the big picture. But he's not great at paperwork. Not at details."

And Sadie had always been marvelous at both. She could organize anything.

"Anyway," she'd reminded her brother. "I didn't stay. I left, remember? I went away to college. Four years at UCLA."

"And then you came back, you idiot. To him."

"To the job," Sadie insisted. "He pays me a mint. And I get a percentage of the business, for heaven's sake. And where else could I possibly go and manage a global property-development business at my age? And still live in Butte?"

"Oh, yeah, that's a real plus. Butte! The hub of the western cultural world."

Of course it was anything but. But the old mining city was making a comeback. Long depressed, Butte was making a slow climb back toward prosperity, thanks in large part to Spence and a few other guys like him who were determined to turn things around.

"Don't be sarcastic. And don't knock Butte." Sadie's voice had been frosty at his dismissal of their hometown. "It's home. Spence doesn't knock it, and he has more right than you do."

She and Danny had had a good childhood with stable, loving parents. Spence had not. For all that he was now a real-estate tycoon of international scope, Spencer Tyack hadn't been born with a silver spoon in his mouth.

"Not even a copper one," he'd once said with a wry grin, a reference to Butte's copper-mining past. "But I survived."

No thanks to his own parents, that was for sure. Sadie remembered Spence's grandfather as kind and caring, but the old man had died when Spence was ten. From then on his life had been hell. His alcoholic father hadn't been able to keep a job and rarely turned up at home except to fight with his mother or take a swing at Spence. And his mother's bitterness toward her husband found its most convenient target in their only son.

Sadie, whom Spence had never permitted to set foot in his house while she was growing up, had still got close enough on occasion to hear her shrieking at him, "You're just like your father!"

He wasn't. Not even close.

Unlike his father, Spence had always been driven. Even when he'd been something of a juvenile delinquent in high school, he'd been determined to be the best delinquent of the bunch.

A probation officer who had insisted they meet not in his office but in the cemetery by Spence's grandfather's grave had put an end to the delinquency. After that Spence had been determined to do the old man proud. To succeed. To achieve. To become the best man he possibly could.

He'd gone to work wherever he could. He'd saved and scrimped and had bought his first house the week he turned twenty-one. To call it a "fixer-upper" would be kind. It had been little more than a hovel with a leaky roof.

As soon as he could, he'd gone to work in the mine, making better money driving those behemoth trucks all day. Then he'd come back and work on the house all night. Several months later he sold that house at a profit, bought another, then did the same. He did it again and again.

By the time he was twenty-two he'd been able to apply for his first commercial-property loan. And that's when he'd hired

Sadie to create order out of the paperwork chaos—in his truck. He hadn't had an office.

"I can't waste money on an office," he'd told her.

So for the first year she'd worked out of the back of his truck camper, using a shop light run by a battery, and a filing system that she carried around in a cardboard box. It was primitive. But it worked.

And so had Spence. Constantly. Within the year he'd had a building. Then two. During her senior year in high school, Sadie finally got an office to call her own. Spence had even bought her a silly plaque that said, "Sadie's office."

And he'd been furious when she'd told him she was leaving to go to college in California.

"I got you an office," he'd protested. "I thought you were going to work for me!"

"Not forever," Sadie had replied.

Because she couldn't. It was more than her sanity was worth, the thought of working for Spence forever—because she was in love with him. Had been for years. As long as she could remember, in fact.

Not that he knew it. God forbid. He'd have been appalled, because he certainly wasn't in love with her.

Sadie knew that. She didn't like it, but she accepted it. She'd tried a little flirting with him, and he'd completely ignored it. So she'd gone to UCLA to get away.

She'd hoped she would learn a lot, get wonderful job offers and meet a man who could make her forget Spence. That had been the plan at least.

And if she'd come home every summer to help Spence out, it was only because he refused to hire anyone in her place while she was gone.

"No need. It can wait for you," he'd said. "You'll be home, anyway."

Which was true. She'd come back to spend summers at her parents' house, to see Gran, to visit Butte. But she hadn't intended to come back permanently. Ever.

Everything went the way she'd planned. She'd learned a lot, graduated with honors and had lots of wonderful job offers—including one from Spence.

He'd come to her graduation. "Why not? I feel like I have a vested interest in your business degree," he'd said blandly. And he'd offered her a job that very afternoon.

He'd promised her a remarkable amount of money, a completely refurbished office in one of Butte's historic landmark buildings that he was painstakingly renovating, and a percentage of his business empire.

"A percentage?" Sadie's eyes had widened in surprise.

But Spence had just shrugged. "Why not? You've worked almost as hard to put Tyack's on the map as I have. You deserve a share. So, what do you say?" The characteristic Tyack impatience was all too clear.

Sadie hadn't known what to say. The truth was she still hadn't gotten over him. His killer grin could still make her knees wobble. His hard-muscled body could still make her quiver all over. And when his steely-eyed stare grew softer and gentler, as it did on rare occasions, her heart seemed to simply turn over in her chest.

She was hopeless, she'd thought grimly. What she needed, she'd decided, was shock therapy. She needed full-scale immersion into Spencer Tyack's world. That would undoubtedly cure her of all her starry-eyed fantasies.

So she'd said yes.

She'd been back for almost six years.

A lot had happened in those six years. She'd done her best to get over him. Told herself she *was* over him. She was dating other men. Just because she hadn't found one yet who set her heart to pounding the way Spence had didn't mean she wouldn't.

She knew Spence wasn't for her.

"I like working for him," she'd told Danny. "It's exciting." Spence was a mover and a shaker. He now had properties in seven countries. He owned apartment complexes, office buildings, condominiums. He always had new ideas. And he always talked about them with her. He sought her opinion. They discussed and analyzed—and argued—together.

"You've got a stake in it," he always said.

And that was true. She did. She might not have a life, but she had a stake in an exciting business. Last week Spence had been in Helsinki finalizing a deal for an office building. This week he was in New York looking over some apartments with father-and-daughter investment team Tom and Dena Wilson, who had done deals with him in the past. And next week, with luck, he would be part owner of a South Pacific resort.

And, as first Danny and now Mr. Isogawa had reminded her, she would be in Butte. Sadie sighed.

It was nearly five. She could leave at five. If she left at five, maybe she would get a life—even though she had piles more work to do.

The phone rang again and unhesitatingly she answered. "Tyack Enterprises. This is Sadie."

"Say-dee, case-me, meu amor." The voice was like rough velvet.

Sadie grinned, recognizing it. If there was ever a man—besides Spence—who could send a woman's hormones into overdrive, Mateus Gonsalves was that man. Trouble was, he knew it. "Hi, Mateus. *Obrigada.* But no, I still don't want to marry you. And Spence is in New York."

He sighed. "I don't want to marry Spence." Mateus Gonsalves switched to perfectly clear, though accented, English. "I want to marry you—and take you away from your slave-driving boss."

It was a conversation they'd had a dozen times at least. From the first time Spence had brought his Brazilian friend to Butte, Mateus had been full of Latin charm, flirting like mad with her, always asking her to marry him.

"She won't," Spence had said cheerfully, not even looking up from the file cabinet he was riffling through. "Sadie's a man-hater."

"I am not!" she'd protested, pushing him out of the way and plucking out at once the document he'd been looking for.

Spence had grabbed it. "See, she's a genius. Knows where everything is," he'd told Mateus happily. Then he'd turned to her. "You don't date."

"I do, too," she'd said. "When the mood hits," she qualified, but that was the truth. She certainly didn't hate men.

"She will date me," Mateus had said with complete assurance.

But she never had. "I don't mix business and pleasure," she'd told him.

"You should," Mateus had rejoined irrepressibly. And he hadn't stopped asking her to come to Rio and marry him every time he called.

"Life is a party in Rio," he said now. "We know how to live down here. You should dump that workaholic and come to work for me."

Sadie laughed at that. "You work almost as hard as he does."

"But I hide it better. And I take holidays. What do you say?"

"Maybe someday I'll come to Rio for a visit," Sadie placated him. "Now, what can I do for you?"

Mateus shifted gears as easily as he always did. "I need to talk to Spencer about a building in Sao Paulo."

"I'll tell him."

"Give me his cell phone number."

"He never turns it on." Unless he was expecting a call, Spence kept his cell phone off. But he always expected her to keep hers on so he could reach her. "When he checks in, I'll have him call you."

"*Obrigado*," he said. "Tell him I've got a proposition for him. And one for you."

"I'm not marrying you, Mateus," she said firmly.

"No marriage," he agreed sadly. "But seriously, Say-dee, you should come work for me. I'm opening an office in Texas. You could run it with one hand tied behind your back."

And have a life besides, Sadie reflected for a brief moment. But then she sighed and shook her head. Battling Mateus off could make life even more difficult than working for Spence who didn't seem to remember that she was a woman. "Thanks. But, no, Mateus."

"Think about it."

"I'll think about it," she agreed because it was easier than arguing with him.

"We will talk later," he promised. "*Adeus, carinha.*"

"*Ciao, Mateus.*" She hung up, then picked up the contracts, determined to take them home and read them. At least that way she could say she'd left the office by ten past five. But her cell phone rang as she did so. She saw who it was and glared.

"It's after five," she said irritably when she picked it up.

"So?" Even when she was annoyed at him, the sound of Spence's rough baritone could cause her pulse to speed up. Damn it.

"I have a life," she snapped.

"Whoa. Who ticked you off?"

You, she wanted to say, even though it was really herself she was annoyed at. "It's been a madhouse here today."

"Well, good. Glad to hear it." Which she supposed he was. "Need you to do something for me," he went on briskly.

Sadie grabbed a pen, ready to write, but he didn't say anything. "Spence?"

"Yeah." He sounded suddenly distracted. His normally quick speech grew even quicker. "No big deal. I just need you to get my birth certificate and the divorce decree and bring them to New York."

Sadie stopped dead. "What?" She felt as if she had been gut-punched. "Do what?"

"You heard me. My birth certificate. The divorce decree. I need them. Tomorrow. In New York."

She'd always thought that breathing was in involuntary reflex. Now she wasn't sure.

"Sadie? Are you there? Did you hear me?" His voice was sharp now.

"I heard you." She managed that much. Couldn't manage any more.

"Great. So just get them and hop on a plane tonight. Or tomorrow. I don't care which. Just so long as you're here by 2:00 p.m."

She didn't speak, just stared mutely at the pencil she'd broken in her hand.

"Sadie!"

"Yes!" she snapped back at him now. "I heard you!"

"Well, good." He paused. "You could congratulate me."

"Because…?" she said, though she knew without asking the reason, even though it stunned her.

"Because I'm getting married." He said the words almost defiantly as if expecting her to argue.

She knew better than to argue. But she couldn't help the sarcasm. "Tomorrow? Isn't that a little precipitous? I mean, considering your track record and all?"

Shut up, she told herself. *Shut up. Shut up. Shut up.*

"It'll be fine this time," he said flatly. "Not like Emily."

"It wasn't Emily I was thinking about," Sadie said, unable to help herself. "You didn't marry Emily."

"I remember who I married." He bit the words out.

Sadie remembered, too. He'd married her!

A wedding on the rebound. When society belle Emily Mollineux had stood him up for their Las Vegas wedding, he'd been gutted. His desperation had reminded Sadie of his boyhood pain when his father walked out and his mother had unleashed her fury on Spence.

So when he'd slammed out of the chapel with a fearsome look in his eyes, Sadie had gone after him, unsure what he might do. She'd never imagined that half a dozen whiskeys later he'd decide the answer was to marry *her!*

But he had. He'd been most insistent. "You'd marry me," he'd said firmly, but there had been just a hint of doubt, the tiniest question in his words, in his gaze. "Wouldn't you?" he'd persisted when she hadn't answered.

And Sadie, because that moment if no other seemed to call for absolute honesty, had to admit she would.

"If you asked me," she'd replied because it was only the truth.

And then, heaven help her, he did.

"Marry me," he'd said. And he'd met her gaze with all the intensity Spencer Tyack was capable of in those midnight eyes.

And so she had married him. Within the hour.

They'd got a license, done the deed. And they'd gone back to the honeymoon suite and made love. Passionately. Desperately. Dazedly. It had been the most amazing night of her life.

And she'd awakened in the honeymoon suite the next morning to find Spence already awake and fully dressed, pacing furiously, raking his hands through his hair and saying, "It was a mistake."

Sadie had barely got her eyes open when he'd come and loomed over her, all harsh expression and anguished bloodshot eyes. "It never should have happened. We never should have— *I* never should have— Hell!" He'd shaken his head as if he didn't believe it. "I'm sorry, Sadie. I never meant— Damn it! I don't know what I was thinking! But it'll be all right. Don't worry. We'll get a divorce."

"A d-divorce?" She'd managed that much. Had simply stared at him slack-jawed.

Spence had nodded vehemently. "Well, we can't get an annulment," he'd said grimly. "But it won't be a problem. I promise. I'll handle it."

He'd been adamant, determined. Just as determined to divorce her as he had been to marry her only twelve hours before. It might be some sort of record, Sadie had remembered thinking. She'd blinked rapidly and tried hard to swallow against the boulder lodged in her throat.

Had it been that awful? That wrong?

Apparently it had.

At least it hadn't seemed like the time to declare her undying love. She'd simply nodded. "Right," she managed, though she'd nearly strangled on the word.

Spence peered at her closely. "Are you okay?"

Oh, yes, terrific. Never better. Having been married and found wanting in the space of half a day was exactly the sort of thing to give a girl a heap of self-confidence!

"I'm fine," she said as steadily as she could. "Why?"

"You don't look fine."

"Thanks very much."

"I didn't mean— I just—" he shuddered visibly "—sorry. I don't know what I was thinking. I'm sorry. Sorry about the marriage. About…" His voice trailed off. His gaze shifted southward, away from her face. Down her sheet-draped body.

Sadie felt immediately self-conscious. So he was sorry they'd consummated the marriage? Sorry he'd made love to her?

He was sorry, apparently, for everything.

"Don't think about it," he said. "I'll handle everything. You don't even have to mention it."

Was he afraid she might? Stand on the rooftops and announce that her husband of twelve hours was dumping her? She stared at him, speechless.

"You're tired. You have to be. Go back to sleep. The room is booked through Wednesday. Stay until then if you want."

As if she would stay on in the honeymoon suite by herself while her husband was divorcing her!

"I won't be here," Spence said quickly, misinterpreting the appalled look on her face. "I called Santiago this morning. I'm just going to head to Barcelona a few days early. But I'll arrange for the divorce before I go. Okay?"

Sadie shrugged. What else could she do?

Seeing the shrug, Spence gave her a strained smile. "It'll be okay. I promise." He paused, then said, "It won't change things, will it? You'll stay on."

"Stay on?"

"Keep working with me. It doesn't have to be awkward. We're friends." He said this last almost insistently and with complete seriousness. And why not? Last night had meant nothing to him—beyond an error in judgment. He wanted her as a friend, not a wife. And he was remedying that as quickly as he could.

She didn't know what to say.

"No" would undoubtedly have been smart. But she had been afraid that saying no would make him think their marriage mattered far more to her than he wanted to believe. And if he thought it did, would he change his mind? Stay married to her because he felt sorry for her?

The very thought made her squirm.

"I'll stay," she said. "For now."

He'd grinned then, that perfect, sexy drop-dead gorgeous

Spencer Tyack grin that Sadie had spent years trying to resist. "That's all right then," he'd said happily. "You're a pal, Sade."

Wasn't she just?

"I knew you'd agree. I'll ring a lawyer from the airport and get him to do it. I'll give you a call tomorrow from Barcelona. But don't worry. Consider it taken care of." And grabbing his suitcase, he'd bolted out the door.

And that, basically, had been that.

Except that when he'd called her from Barcelona the next day, he'd said, "Are you okay?" in a worried tone completely unlike any he'd ever used with her.

"Of course I'm okay. What do you think?" Sadie had retorted. She was damned if she was going to let him think he'd cut her heart out.

She must have been convincing because he'd never asked that question or sounded that worried again. And the first morning he was back in the office, which was a month later, he'd said, "Don't worry. It's sorted. I've got the papers. It's all taken care of."

And so her short, better-forgotten marriage to Spence had been over.

He'd never mentioned it again.

Neither had she. She'd thought of it again, of course. Plenty of times in those first few months. Minute by minute almost. But eventually she'd managed to put it aside. Not to forget, but to consider it with detachment, as if it had happened in some alternative universe. Like a dream. Or a nightmare.

It had faded over the past four years. Until now. Now she said, "I don't know where the papers are."

"In my safe deposit box. You have a key."

"Yes, but—married?"

"It's business, Sadie. Did you think I'd fallen in love?"

She didn't know what to think. "Business?"

"I'm marrying Dena Wilson. Who'd you think I was marrying? Someone I just picked up on the street?"

"I—"

"It's perfect. A great idea. Dena and I joining forces. I don't know why I didn't think of it sooner. Together we've got twice the clout. Twice the expertise."

"Yes, but—tomorrow?"

"So we'll be married before I head to Fiji. Which reminds me, can you book a flight for Dena?"

She was going to kill him.

"You don't have to do it tonight," he said, all magnanimity. "You can do it tomorrow from here. Just bring the papers and show up at the courthouse tomorrow afternoon. Ceremony's at two. I'll book you a room in a fancy hotel for tomorrow night for your trouble, okay? The Plaza? The Four Seasons? You name it. Think of it as a vacation. Right. I've got to run. Tom and Dena just came in the door. See you tomorrow."

There was a click—and a second later, a dial tone.

Sadie stood staring at the phone in her hand and felt as if the bottom had fallen out of her well-ordered world.

Where the hell was she?

Spence checked his watch for the tenth time in five minutes and raked fingers through his already disheveled hair. He'd been pacing the hallway of the courthouse, just outside the judge's chamber for three-quarters of an hour.

He'd got there an hour before that, wanting to be there when Sadie showed up and not certain when she would arrive. Last night he'd kept his phone off, not wanting to get any calls from Sadie telling him he was making a mistake.

He wasn't making a mistake.

The Emily fiasco had been a mistake. No doubt about that. Four years ago when he'd intended to marry Emily Mollineux,

he'd been out of his mind—a victim of his own youthful enthusiasm, infatuation and hormones—not to mention a mis-
placed determination to wed a beauty whose family was all
about Old Money.

And marrying Sadie for God-knew-what insane reason
after Emily hadn't shown up—well, that had been an even
bigger mistake.

He should never have imposed on her, never proposed!
Never put her on the spot like that.

But at the moment he'd been out of his mind. Insane.
Rejected. The word still made him wince. But Emily's defection had seemed to confirm his deepest fears—that, as his
mother had always claimed, he was worthless.

And so he'd turned to Sadie—had used her unwavering
friendship to restore, however briefly, his shattered self-esteem.
It had been easy enough to do, damn it. For all that she would
argue with him forever about business propositions, Sadie was
putty when it came to people—when it came to him.

And in the morning when he'd awakened to find her in bed
beside him, when he remembered how they'd spent the night,
he'd been appalled at what he'd done.

Christ, she'd even had a boyfriend! And he hadn't given a
damn.

He'd just turned to her and said, "Marry me," and he knew
that that night he wouldn't—couldn't—have taken no for an
answer. But in the morning's harsh light he knew regret. He
knew he'd made a mistake.

And so he'd done his best to make it right.

He wasn't making that mistake again. This marriage was
business, pure and simple. He and Dena both wanted exactly
the same things. It would be fine.

Provided, he thought, shooting back his cuff and glaring at
his watch again, Sadie showed up.

He didn't know where she was or what time her flight had been expected to get in. He might have known, he reminded himself, if he'd turned on his mobile phone last night. But he hadn't. He hadn't wanted to talk to her last night—just in case she tried to talk him out of this marriage.

Sadie was, after all, an idealist, a romantic. As long as he'd known her, she'd been deluded by the notion that someday she would meet "the one." It was one of the reasons he'd known he had to divorce her as quickly as possible—to give her a chance to meet her Perfect Man.

So he hadn't wanted to hear how Dena Wilson wasn't his Perfect Woman. She was all about business—not at all about home and family. She didn't want them any more than he did. And that, to Spence, was about as perfect as she could get.

So he'd shut his phone off and, consequently, he had no idea where the hell Sadie was or when to expect her. He'd tried calling her, but her own phone was shut off.

He knew, of course, that if she was still in the air, she couldn't have it switched on. But good God, she'd better not be in the air now. The ceremony was due to start in less than fifteen minutes.

"Well, Sadie is certainly cutting it a little close," Dena said, appearing at his side. She was smiling her usually imperturbable smile, but there was a hint of strain around her mouth.

"She'll be here."

"Of course. Just give me a heads up. I have some papers to go over," Dena said. "I'll work on them."

She went back into the room, and Spence continued to pace the hallway. He cracked his knuckles. He tried her number again. And again.

Ten minutes later the door to the judge's chambers opened and Dena's father, Tom, appeared. "I'm meeting Sawyer in Savannah at nine. Let's get this show on the road."

"Sadie's not here."

"You're not marrying Sadie."

"She's bringing my papers. Birth certificate. Divorce decree." He hadn't wanted to mention the divorce, but of course he'd had to.

Dena had raised her eyebrows at the news, but then she'd shrugged. "Makes no difference to me."

"Get married now. Worry about the paperwork after." Tom suggested.

"Without Sadie?"

"Why not? No big deal, is it?" Tom said with the air of a man who bent the rules to meet the circumstances. He checked his watch pointedly.

Spence shrugged. "Of course not."

It was sensible. Sane. Logical. It was making the best use of time and resources—just as their marriage would be.

As Mr. and Mrs. Spencer Tyack, they would improve their business standing enormously. Dena's considerable assets alongside his would add to their portfolio and their viability on the property-development front in the long run. And in the short run it would solve a problem with Mr. Isogawa and his "happy family" scenario. One of Spence's partners had a wife with a wandering eye. In Barcelona last month it—and she— had wandered in Spence's direction. Into his bedroom, in fact.

The last thing he needed was her pulling a stunt like that at the resort. Having a wife along, he'd determined, would make sure it didn't happen.

He understood that Tadahiro Isogawa was, as Sadie had said, all about happy families. So was he, even though his personal experience of them was negligible. Marrying Dena, though, could solve his problem and create enormous opportunities for them in the future. He could certainly be happy about that.

And Dena, when he proposed the idea, had understood at once.

"Smart," she'd said after only brief consideration. "We'll do it—for the business. And sex, of course. But no kids. Those are my terms."

"No problem," Spence had agreed promptly. Those were his terms, too.

So here they were now—all of them, except Sadie.

Where the hell was she?

"So, are we ready?" Tom said briskly.

"Sure. Why not?"

Tom smiled. "I'll get Dena."

The clerk went to get the judge. Tom reappeared moments later with Dena, still carrying her briefcase. Spence put his suit coat back on and straightened his tie.

The door opened and the judge swept in. "I'm in recess," he announced. "Not much time." He glanced at Spence and Dena. "You're the couple? Come up here."

Spence took Dena's arm and went to stand in front of the judge, who cleared his throat and began to speak rapidly in a monotone. It was all legalese. Mumbo-jumbo. Not real estate law so Spence didn't understand any of it. It didn't matter. What mattered was saying "I do," at the right moment. And finding Sadie.

Suddenly he heard a door squeaking open behind them. His head whipped around.

Sadie!

But hardly the calm, centered, settled Sadie he'd been expecting. This Sadie's hair was windblown, her eyes bloodshot with dark circles beneath. Her skin was so pale that her normally golden freckles seemed to have been splashed across her cheeks by an impressionist run amok. And the look she gave him was of a deer caught in the headlights of a semi. A deer clutching a red leather portfolio against her chest.

"Don't just stand there, young woman!" the judge barked. "Sit down! I don't have all day."

"I need to—"

"Shut the door and sit!"

Sadie shut the door and sat.

Clearing his throat, the judge began again. More legalese. Something about the power vested in him by the state of New York. Blah, blah, blah. Behind him Spence heard someone— Sadie?—fidget in her chair.

"…must ascertain if there are any legal impediments or reasons why this marriage should not take place. Any objections?" Then without pausing, the judge continued, "No. So we'll move on then and—"

"Yes." It was Sadie.

Spence jerked around to stare at her. So did Dena and Tom.

"You object, young woman?" the judge demanded.

"I, um, yes."

The judge's brows drew down. "On what grounds may I ask?"

What the hell was she playing at? Spence scowled furiously at her.

Sadie shot one quick unreadable glance at him, then turned her gaze back to the judge again. "He's already married. To me."

CHAPTER TWO

"WHAT!" Spence stared at her.

The judge's jaw sagged, Tom Wilson's eyes bugged, Dena's mouth flew open, and Sadie understood perfectly. She'd done all of the above.

Now she wet her lips and made a faint and fairly unsuccessful attempt to smile. "I'm afraid it's true," she said apologetically to the judge and Tom and Dena. But by the time her gaze reached Spence, she hoped there was no apology left in it at all.

"What are you talking about? That was years ago! The divorce papers—"

"We need to talk about that," Sadie said. And she hoped they had reached the point in their years-long relationship where nonverbal communication was a no-brainer.

"Damned right we do," Spence said. He shot a quick glance at Dena—also apologetic, Sadie noted—and one that seemed to say, "you just can't get good help these days," to the judge and Tom. And then he stalked over and took her arm none too gently. "Come on."

"Don't be long. I've got a plane to catch," Tom called after them.

Spence didn't reply. He hustled her out of the room and into the hallway, looked around at the various people in the corridor and opened the door to a room across the way. "In here." He kicked the door shut behind them, then spun her around to face him. "What the hell do you think you're doing?"

"Trying to stop you committing bigamy," she suggested.

"Don't be ridiculous. That was hardly a marriage we had and—"

"It was quite legal in the state of Nevada."

"And I filed for divorce the next day."

"Correction," Sadie said, "you called a divorce lawyer and told him to handle it."

"Which he did! I got the papers!"

"You got an envelope," Sadie corrected him. "You didn't open it." Which was pretty much Spence all over. Delegate and assume it would be done.

Too bad he hadn't delegated arranging their divorce to *her!*

Spence's jaw tightened. "I didn't want to look at them," he growled. "Would you?"

"No." She had to admit she wouldn't have wanted to see their folly in black-and-white, either. It had been far too painful in those days. "But I would have made sure it was done."

He shook his head. "So what was that?" He frowned as she withdrew the envelope from her portfolio. It was a bright-red portfolio, one he had bought her after she'd complained that she couldn't find things in her office if he came in and dumped papers on them.

"Put them in here," he'd said, brandishing the shocking-red leather case. "You won't mislay them, then."

Sadie forbore telling him she never mislaid anything, he just covered things up. Instead she'd thanked him—and made good use of it. Now she took the papers out of the envelope and showed them to him. The first one was the cover letter thanking him for contacting them and telling him they would be happy to handle the case if he would simply fill in the forms enclosed and create a Nevada residence which he needed to maintain for six weeks before filing. Another six weeks after, and if the divorce was uncontested, it would be finalized.

"No problem," the letter had concluded. "We are specialists at correcting such mistakes and we will file your papers as soon as you verify your Nevada address and fill in the necessary forms."

Spence stared at them. He flipped through them. Read them once—and then again. And then he lifted his gaze. He looked furious. "Bloody hell." He slammed the papers down on the desk and spun away, prowling the room. "They could have called! Did they think I'd changed my mind?"

"That is apparently exactly what they thought," Sadie told him. "I rang them this morning."

It had been too late last night by the time she'd gone to the bank and searched for the papers he wanted. She'd found his birth certificate right away. But the divorce papers weren't there. In desperation she'd opened the only thing she thought they could be in—the unopened envelope from a Las Vegas law firm. And when she'd read the letter, she'd stood there stunned, realizing that Spence had never read it, hadn't even bothered to open it.

And then, she, too, had thought that surely he must have had some other contact with them.

"I called the courthouse to check, when I didn't find the papers. They said there was no divorce on file. By then it was too late to call the lawyer. So I did it this morning on my layover." That had been another disaster—a plane with mechanical problems that had landed for an unscheduled maintenance stop in Detroit. But at least she'd been able to confirm her worst suspicion.

"They checked their records. They had nothing beyond a note of your initial phone message. They said it happens more often than you would think," she added, "people changing their minds."

Spence just stared at her.

Sadie shrugged. "So, it appears we are still married."

The notion had had her brain buzzing all night. *Married?* She was still *married?* To *Spence?*

"Bloody hell," Spence said again, then raked a hand through his hair so it stood up in dark spikes all over his head.

Good thing she hadn't expected him to be thrilled. "Sorry," she said with some asperity. "I realize it upsets your plans."

"Damned right it does." He ground his teeth, then sighed. "Not your fault," he muttered grudgingly. He slanted her a glance. "You would have seen it was done."

"Yes," Sadie agreed.

They stared at each other. In his gaze Sadie could see he knew it was true.

"But I didn't want to put you to the trouble," he muttered. "It was my screwup. My mistake."

"I'd say we both made a mistake," Sadie replied. She, after all, had been idiot enough to agree.

There was a light knock on the door. Before either of them could say, "Come in," it opened and Tom poked his head around the door. "Sorted?" he asked Spence.

Spence shook his head. "We have a small…hang-up."

"How small?"

"Not very," Spence said grimly.

Tom's eyes widened. He looked at Sadie. "You're still married to her?" His astonishment—and disapproval—were obvious.

"So it seems. Just go to your meeting, Tom. I'll talk to Dena. We'll sort things out."

"But the wedding—"

"Is off. For now."

"But what about the island resort project?" asked Tom. "What about Carstairs? Leonie? What will Isogawa say?"

Sadie frowned at these references to the people she had just lined up to attend the meeting at Nanumi. What did they have to do with his marriage?

"What *about* the island resort project?" she asked. "What about Mr. Isogawa and Richard and Leonie Carstairs?"

"Why? What do you know about Leonie?" Spence demanded, fixing her with a hard look, as if he thought she'd been prying.

"Nothing," Sadie said. "Well, nothing much," she corrected herself. "She just seems a little insecure."

Both men stared at her.

"She keeps ringing me," Sadie said, "very worried that Richard will come to the meeting without her. I assured her he wouldn't, that Mr. Isogawa wants couples, that she'd be very welcome."

Spence's jaw tightened. Tom gave him an arch look that Sadie didn't understand.

"She would be," Sadie said. "Mr. Isogawa said wives were welcome. Encouraged, in fact." Was that why he'd wanted to bring Dena? But she couldn't ask—not in front of Dena's father. Even though Tom Wilson was as much of a businessman as Spence, it didn't seem like the thing to say.

"Right," Spence muttered. "It's just—never mind." He broke off and turned to the other man. "Just go on now, Tom. I'll be in touch."

"What about Dena? What are you going to tell my daughter?"

"I'll explain."

Tom just looked at him doubtfully, then shook his head. "If this blows up—"

"It won't."

Tom looked doubtful. But Sadie knew that Spence didn't do doubt. He stared Tom down until finally the latter pressed his lips together and gave a curt nod. "Fine. Handle it, then." And he was gone.

In his absence there was silence.

"We can get a divorce," Sadie felt compelled to say.

"Not in the next half hour."

"Well, no. But—"

"Forget it. For now," Spence amended. "I need to talk to Dena."

"I'll come with you."

"No, you won't."

"But—"

"No. This is between me and Dena. Our wedding may have been business, but she's my friend. And I owe her the courtesy of telling her what's going on personally. Privately."

"I just thought it might help if—"

"It wouldn't," he said harshly. "And I think you've helped enough for one day, Sadie. Just wait here. I'll be back." And he stalked out the door, banging it shut behind him.

She'd helped? As if this were all her fault?

Well, it wasn't. But some of it was. She needed to make a break. She would see about the divorce this time—and get it done properly. And then she would leave. Find a new job. Sell Spence back his percentage of the company. That would certainly make it permanent. She needed to stop waffling around, trying to make a life for herself while all the while she hovered on the edge of Spence's.

Enough Spence.

There would be a time, as Danny had said, when she would finally need to grow up and take control of her life—to *get* a life.

"And the time," she told herself firmly, "is now."

Dena didn't even look up when he came into the judge's chambers. She was reading some legal documents, completely absorbed. No one looking at her would ever have imagined she'd just had her wedding cut out from under her. As always, she was immaculate and composed. Not a blond hair was out of place. The lipstick she'd put on right before the ceremony still looked fresh, not gnawed.

Spence, on the other hand, felt as if he'd been dragged through the New York subway system backward and shot point-blank with a stun gun.

He was *married?* To *Sadie?* Had been married to her for the past four years?

Dena finished the page she was reading before she looked up at him expectantly and smiled her own cool, self-possessed smile. "Well," she said. "That was interesting."

He knew she didn't mean the papers in her hand. His jaw clenched and he had to make an effort to relax it. "Yes." But he couldn't keep from biting the word off, and apparently that was the only clue she needed.

"So, it's true?"

"Apparently." He explained haltingly. Not about Emily. He just said he and Sadie had been in Vegas. They'd got married. In the morning he'd realized it was a mistake. It was hard not to sound like an idiot. So he tried not to go into too much detail, just hoped that sane matter-of-fact words came out of his mouth until finally there seemed nothing more to say.

"Obviously, I should have read the damn letter. I assumed it was a done deal."

Dena let the silence gather for a few seconds before she said mildly, "That'll teach you," as if it were only a minor folly, not a full-scale disaster.

"It will," Spence said. His jaw locked tight. His head pounded.

"So, okay. As long as we know," Dena said, shifting gears. "I just don't want to see the deal fall through."

He stared at her, surprised that she was taking it so calmly. But then, he reminded himself, it was just business to her. Business deals collapsed all the time. And in any case, it was his problem, not hers.

"It'll be fine," she said. "You just take Sadie instead."

"What?" Spence stared at her.

Dena gave him a completely guileless look. "Well, she's your wife."

"Yes, but—" He couldn't finish. It would never be "just business" with Sadie. It couldn't be.

Sadie was businesslike, but she didn't see the world the same way he did.

"Well, what else are you going to do?" Dena said reasonably. "It won't look very good to Isogawa and his 'happy family' theme if you show up having just filed for divorce."

"No." He was trying to think. He was usually so damn good at it. Solutions were always at his fingertips, always on the tip of his tongue.

"You've worked too long, too hard on this resort. It's a once-in-a-lifetime opportunity," Dena reminded him.

"I know that," Spence said tersely. There were bigger investors in the deal—Richard Carstairs for one—but Spence was the one who had made the initial contact with Mr. Isogawa. He was the one whose reputation was riding on it. Richard and John and Steve, the other three investors, were old hands at this sort of deal. This was Spence's first resort, first foray into business in the Pacific. He had more stake in it than anyone.

"So you have to make it work," Dena said simply. "And if once upon a time you couldn't keep your jeans zipped and Sadie made you make an honest woman of her, so be it. At least you're married. That's what's important."

Spence barely heard the last part. His brain had ground to a screeching halt at the words *You couldn't keep your jeans zipped*.

All of a sudden memories of a naked Sadie Morrissey were alive and well and rising like a phoenix in his brain.

He pressed his palms to the sides of his head, feeling as if it were going to explode.

"What's wrong?" Dena asked. "Headache? I wouldn't be surprised."

"No. Yeah. I need to think."

"Yes. And thank your lucky stars Sadie showed up."

Spence blinked, then goggled at her. "Lucky?"

"Well, it certainly wouldn't have done any good if you'd turned out to be a bigamist, would it?" Dena said impatiently. "With Isogawa being Mr. Propriety. Let's face it, if he'd discovered you were married to two women, the deal would be in the trash faster than you can say 'bigamist.' And Leonie would have been thrilled. She might have steered clear of you seeing one wedding ring on your finger. But I'm pretty sure two would have allowed her to put her scruples aside." She smiled.

Spence didn't. He was usually pretty good at taking whatever life dealt him and making the best of it.

But he couldn't see how he was going to make the best of being married to Sadie Morrissey.

Dena kept smiling. "You'll be fine. You wanted a wife, didn't you?"

"Yes, but—"

"You've got one. And she knows your business. You'll be fine. Just do what you do best."

He looked at her blankly.

She stood up, put the papers away, then closed her briefcase and patted him on the cheek as she turned toward the door. "Improvise."

Sadie could hear Spence bellowing her name up and down the hallway.

It was tempting to stay right where she was—in the ladies' room. But that would be cowardly, and she'd faced the worst already, hadn't she?

Of course she had. Now they just had to sit down and work out how to get divorced for real. She could do that. And Spence would *want* to do it. He had probably already filled out the paperwork.

"So get on with it," she told herself. "Nothing's changed."

Not really. It wasn't like they were a real couple who had loved each other. She had loved him—still did, she supposed. But that had been foolish. She should have tried harder to get over it. She should have left years ago.

Well, better late than never, she thought. That was what Gran always said. She sent a prayer winging heavenward, a little divine help—or a little encouragement from Gran— wouldn't come amiss right now.

Please, she added as she pushed open the door and stepped out.

Spence was standing with his back to her, punching his cell phone furiously. Then he raised it to his ear and waited. Tapped his foot. Ran his fingers through his hair.

Sadie approached quietly, knowing better than to interrupt his call.

He glared at the phone, punched another button furiously, then snarled into it, "Damn it, Sadie. Where the hell are you?"

"Right behind you."

He whipped around. He glared at her, then at the phone. Then he flicked it shut and stuck it in his pocket. "Where have you been?"

"I went to the ladies' room while you were talking to Dena. Is she all right?"

"Who? Dena?"

"Of course. Was she very upset?"

"Not a bit." He shrugged as if it didn't matter, but there was an edge of annoyance in his voice. Had their proposed marriage, perhaps, not been totally business, after all?

Sadie didn't want to think about that. She'd always liked Dena, and among the many reasons she'd hated having to announce their marriage so bluntly today was the worry that, despite Spence's assurances to the contrary, Dena might really be hurt. "I'm so glad. I wouldn't have wanted to hurt her."

"Hurt her? What about me?" Spence said indignantly.

"It was just business for you!"

"My business could be hurt."

"How?" Sadie cocked her head. "Were you counting on maybe a Caribbean island from Daddy for a wedding present?"

"No, I damned well was not!" His indignation was very real now, and Sadie felt small for having made the remark.

In his entire life Spencer Tyack had never got anything the easy way. No one had given him anything. And it had always been a matter of honor for him to earn everything he had.

"Sorry," Sadie said now and meant it. "I'm sure it's…difficult. And for all that it was business," she added quickly, "you must care. We'll get a divorce as quick as we can and then you can marry Dena."

"No," he said flatly. "I can't."

"Why not?"

"Because I'd have to divorce you first."

"Well, yes, but—"

"And Isogawa's not going to like that. He's as old school as they come. He believes in the sanctity and stability of marriage."

"So do I," Sadie muttered. "Appearances to the contrary."

"You shouldn't have said yes, then," Spence snapped. He looked as if he'd like to hit something.

No, she certainly shouldn't have. But it was too late for self-recrimination now. "Fine," she said. "If you don't want to get a divorce right now, we won't. We can wait until you're back. Until your deal is done. Isogawa doesn't have to know. After all, until less than an hour ago, *you* didn't know! Let him go on thinking you're single."

"Can't."

"Oh, for God's sake, stop being cryptic! Why can't you?" Sadie scowled, perplexed by his stubbornness. "I've talked to him. Yes, he's very into marriage and family. But he doesn't think the whole world has to march two by two." She knew enough of Mr. Isogawa's views to be sure of that.

But Spence just shook his head. "No. Look, I—" He started as if he were going to explain further, but then looked around at the people wandering up and down the corridor, some of them giving the two of them speculative looks, and instead abruptly he took her by the arm.

"I don't want to discuss this here," he said. "Let's get a cab."

"A cab? And go where?"

"To my place." And as he spoke he steered her toward the elevator.

His place? Sadie knew, of course, that he had a pied-à-terre on the Upper West Side. In the past two years, he'd spent so much time in New York that he kept a studio apartment here as well as one in the Caribbean, one in Greece and one in Spain. Sadie had seen pictures of them all, but she'd never been to any in person. In fact she could count on the fingers of a single hand the occasions that she had ever been in Spence's house in Butte!

For all that she had grown up with him running in and out of her house with Danny, the reverse had never been true.

When they'd been children, life in Spence's house—with his bitter mother and unreliable father—had been unpredictable at best. She knew he hadn't wanted anyone to witness it.

But even now that he was master of his own destiny and domain, and lived in one of the old Copper King mansions he'd restored himself in uptown Butte, Spence kept his home separate from the rest of his life.

"It's the way he is." Danny had shrugged with complete indifference when Sadie had asked him about it. "Besides," he'd added with patently bossy big-brotherliness, "you don't want to go there."

Which hadn't been true at all.

Being seriously infatuated with him, Sadie had wanted to very much. But in all the years she had known him and worked for him, Spence had remained a good employer—and a good friend—but a man with definite boundaries.

"You're taking me to your place?" she echoed now, surprised.

"Where the hell else," he said gruffly, "since you're my wife."

He could snarl the words "my wife" easily enough. It was less easy to think about the reality of it. In fact, it was damn near impossible.

Spence sat in the backseat of the taxi carrying them to his Upper West Side apartment and studied Sadie out of the corner of his eye.

His "wife" was sitting in the backseat, too, but as far away from him as she could get, as if she were trying to avoid contamination. She wasn't looking his way, either. Instead she was deliberately staring out the window, feigning complete absorption in the traffic as they hurtled, then crawled, up Eighth Avenue.

That wasn't like Sadie. Sadie usually paid no attention at all to where they were. She was normally focused on him, waving papers in his face, pointing at fine print, rattling on a mile a minute.

Now she wasn't saying a word.

Of course, he knew she wasn't happy, either. This situation—this mess!—was no more normal for her than it was for him, though she'd had a few hours longer to get used to it.

What was she thinking? Usually he had no trouble figuring that out. Usually she was telling him without his having to ask. It was what they did—discuss, argue, debate, clarify.

But now she was as still and silent as a stone. He wished he could see inside her head. Then again, all things considered, it was probably better he couldn't.

This was all his fault. No doubt about it.

He accepted that. Spence was never one to deny responsibility. He should have made sure it was taken care of. Should have faced his demons and his momentary foolishness and made sure it didn't come back to haunt them.

But he hadn't. His mistake.

So it was his job to fix it. Properly. Completely. Unflinchingly.

And he would.

But first he had to deal with the resort. They'd worked too long and too hard on it—both he and Sadie—to risk letting the deal fall apart now. He wasn't sure exactly how to handle it, though. His intuition, normally brilliant—if he did say so himself—seemed to have completely deserted him.

Dena's notion—that he take Sadie—was impossible. She would never agree. And he understood completely. But he couldn't think of any other options.

Sadie would. He was sure. That was the joy of having her working with him. They battled things out. He proposed and she contradicted. Usually he was right, or close enough. But sometimes she had a better idea.

She'd better have a better idea today.

He started to say something, then shut his mouth again. He didn't want to start the argument in the taxi. So he would wait. He would get her back to his place and then he would tell her what they needed to do.

And she could argue him around to something else. Yeah. He smiled at the thought, the first smile he'd managed since Sadie had dropped her bombshell an hour ago. Then he shifted against the back of the seat, flexed his rigid shoulders, took a deep breath and felt considerably better.

They finished the cab ride in silence. When they reached his apartment, Spence paid off the driver and gestured her ahead of him up the stairs to the brownstone in which he owned a floor-through apartment.

He unlocked the door and said, "Third floor," and waited until she started up the steps, then fell in behind her.

"You don't have to bring up my case," Sadie said.

Spence didn't bother to reply. He wasn't getting them sidetracked on another argument. Instead he just jerked his head toward the stairs. Sadie scowled at him, but began to climb.

He went up after her—and found himself at eye level with a curvy female backside that sparked a memory. He tried to resist it.

But his eyes were glued to the view—and the word *wife* was suddenly pounding in his brain. Not just *wife* but *my wife*.

He hadn't seen Sadie as a woman in years—hadn't let himself even consider her that way, except obviously for one very intense night. And now, damn it, was not the time to start!

So he stopped where he was and let her get half a dozen steps ahead of him.

Sadie glanced back over her shoulder. "Something wrong? I told you not to lug it up. It's heavy."

Did she think he couldn't carry her damned suitcase? "It's fine," Spence snapped. "I've got…something in my shoe. Go on."

Sadie raised skeptical eyebrows, but shrugged, then turned and kept on going. Spence waited until she had reached the next landing and had disappeared from view. Only then, when he was no longer treated to a vision of her backside, did he continue up after her.

Wordlessly he unlocked the door and pushed it open, then waved her in ahead of him.

"Not going to carry me over the threshold?"

He stared at her. "Do you want me to?"

"No! Of course not." She scurried into the apartment. "I'm

just being—" she grimaced, then gave him a quick self-conscious smile and a little awkward shrug "—inappropriate."

Spence followed her in and kicked the door shut behind him. "Not as inappropriate as you might think," he said, dropping her suitcase on the floor.

Sadie frowned. "What do you mean?"

"I mean that, as apparently we're still married, on Friday you're coming to Nanumi with me—as my wife."

CHAPTER THREE

GO WITH him to Nanumi? As his wife?

Sadie stared.

"Why not?" Spence persisted. He began pacing around the room. It was a small room, relatively impersonal, exactly the sort of anonymous place she'd expected he would have. "We're married. You said so."

"Yes. I did. But—" She looked at him more closely. Was he suggesting…? Surely he couldn't mean…?

Her heart seemed to kicked over in her chest as her brain entertained a possibility that had never occurred to her—that Spence would want to continue their "marriage", that he saw her as a woman at last.

He stopped dead square in front of her. "For better or worse, Sadie," he said, as if she needed the reminder, "right now you're my wife. And Isogawa is all about family. You said so yourself. He wants couples at the resort. We're a couple. It makes perfect sense. Right?" He was grinning now, looming over her, daring her to contradict him, to argue.

And Sadie suddenly knew it had nothing to do with wanting to stay married to her at all. He wanted to argue.

This was Spence in confrontation mode. Spence looking for a fight. A challenge. It was the way he worked.

Spence's gut-level instinct picked up and proposed things continually. Sometimes, Sadie thought, his brain worked faster than the speed of light.

It was the way he began each deal. He would spot a possibility, then—using some sort of sixth sense, some intuition that she could never quite catch up with—he would analyze whatever he was considering at warp speed, consider the options, calculate the odds, then fling some sort of outrageous idea at her.

Like now.

Usually, of course, he didn't do it with the edgy fierceness she heard in his voice now, despite the grin. But even with the granite-jawed, I-eat-sharks-for-breakfast glitter in his eyes, the look on his face was decidedly familiar.

He was daring her to confront him, to stop him. He didn't expect her to agree. He was, to put it bluntly, looking for a fight.

And, she was quite sure now, hoping she would provide him with half a dozen other options. It was the way they worked. One of Spence's tests of his intuition, Sadie had realized long ago, was to spring a decision on her, then wait for her to argue.

And Sadie always embraced the opportunity. She loved arguing with Spence. It excited her, exhilarated her. It made her feel as if she were a vital part of his decision-making process, a real member of the team, because Spence really did listen to what she said. And he was, if she was convincing enough, quite willing to revise and reconsider as a result of their battles.

Now she just smiled and said, "All right."

The sudden silence in the room was deafening. Spence stared at her, eyes wide. "*All right?* What the hell do you mean, *all right?*"

"I mean, I agree."

His dark brows drew down, and he scowled furiously at her as he rubbed a hand against the back of his neck. "I wasn't asking you," he said sharply. "I was telling you."

"Yes. And I agreed with you."

"You do? I mean, of course you do," he blustered. "It only makes sense."

Sadie nodded. "Yes."

"You think so?" He was eyeing her narrowly.

What made real sense, Sadie thought, was for her to turn tail and run for the hills. She wasn't used to Spence looking at her like that—with that intense gleam in his eye. But she'd backed down, gentled, calmed and gone on far too much in the past. It was time to stop, for her own sake as much as his.

"Yes," she said firmly, "I do."

"Why?"

She shook her head. She wasn't telling him that. She wasn't even sure she had worked out all the reasons yet herself. But she knew what she had to say.

"It's just business."

He blinked. Then nodded. "Yes."

"So, no big deal." Hahaha, her brain chortled at her naiveté, but she ignored it. "I'll go to Fiji with you. And after, I'll resign. I'll come home. We'll get the divorce. A real one this time—with paperwork completed. All i's dotted and t's crossed. Official. Legal. And then I'll get out of your life."

"Don't be ridiculous. I mean, the divorce, yeah. Sure. Fine. But you don't have to get out of my life!"

"Yes, I do."

Dear God, yes, she absolutely did. She certainly did not want go through this again, get *another* divorce from Spencer Tyack and then go back to being his office manager. She'd been foolish enough and self-deluded enough to try it once. And to a degree it had worked. But she hadn't ever got over him. And if she stayed she never would.

She looked up and met his eyes with as steady a gaze as she could manage.

"I'll be your wife for the week. And then I'm gone."

Spence's jaw tightened. He glared at her for a long time, then shrugged. "Suit yourself."

"I am."

It would, she decided, serve her right. She would go to Nanumi with him as his real, honest-to-God wife for a week. And she would let herself act like a wife. She would have a week of the dream that she'd always wanted. And then she would leave. There would undoubtedly be a bit of shock value in it. Maybe it would wake her up sufficiently to force her to get on with her life.

Spence didn't look completely convinced. And she wasn't going to stand there and argue with him about it now.

"I'm filthy," she said. "And I've been up all night. I need a shower. May I take one?"

He looked startled. His scowl deepened. "A shower? Here?"

"You have a bath, I think. Indoor plumbing? I know I've never been to New York before, but surely—"

"Yes, damn it." He jerked his head toward a door beyond the small kitchen area. "Go for it."

"Thank you." She shrugged, glad now to have her suitcase and fresh clothes at hand. "I've been on the road since yesterday evening."

"Then why were you late?"

"Plane trouble. We had a wiring problem. Spent five hours on the ground in Detroit. Just think, if the plane had gone down, you would have been a widower and all would have been well." She smiled up at him brightly from where she knelt and opened her suitcase.

"Don't be an ass!" Spence snapped.

She was trying hard not to be. She pulled out a pair of linen slacks, a scoop-necked T-shirt and some clean underthings, and got a grip on her wayward emotions. Only when she was sure she was in control again, did she stand up to face him.

He was standing in her way, staring at her. "Do you mind?" she pressed when he didn't move. "A shower?" His gaze seemed fixed on the clothes in her arms and she wasn't even sure he'd heard her. "Spence?"

He gave a quick shake of his head. "No, of course I don't mind." And as if he suddenly realized why she wasn't moving—because she couldn't—he moved out of her way.

"Thank you." She slipped past him. "I'll hurry."

"Take your time," he muttered. "I'll get…us some food."

"Sounds good," she lied, certain she couldn't eat a thing. She went into the bathroom, then turned and gave him one last bright determined smile.

He was still staring at her when she closed the door.

Sadie wore silk underwear!

Those were peach-colored silk panties she had in her hands, not to mention a lacy scrap of a bra that looked as if it had come right out of some Hollywood lingerie catalog. Not the sort of underwear she could have bought in Butte!

Spence's mind went straight from the sight of those lacy garments in Sadie's arms to a vision of her wearing them. He sucked air.

The unexpectedness of it had him gasping. Not just the un-expectedness of the peach-colored lace and silk—which was astonishing enough given Sadie's sensible matter-of-fact demeanor—but even more his brain's almost immediate and very vivid notion of what she would look like wearing it.

Somewhere back in Sadie's teenage years, Spence had begun to notice that Danny's kid sister wasn't built like a stick insect anymore. He'd even found himself, more than once, lying in bed thinking about her curvy body and her long long legs and ima-gining what they'd be like bare and wrapped around his waist.

One night he'd actually made a remark about her feminine

attributes in front of Danny—and found himself knocked off the bar stool.

"Don't even think it," Danny had warned, standing over him, breathing hard. "Sadie's the marrying kind. Or she will be when she's old enough. She's a good girl and she's going to stay that way. So you keep your eyes—and hands—off and your zipper welded shut. She's not for the likes of you! Got it?"

Spence had got it.

And even in his hormone-driven lust-filled early twenties he had known that Danny was right. Sadie *was* a great girl. A good girl. And when she grew up, she would deserve a good man. The best.

God knew that wasn't him. With his alcoholic, here-today gone-tomorrow father and his bitter hard mother, not to mention the chip he carried on his shoulder that was the size of all the rock they'd ever taken out of the Berkeley Pit, Spencer Tyack was no man for a girl like Sadie Morrissey.

So he had kept his hands to himself—and his zipper, around Sadie at least, firmly zipped. But he had still known she was gorgeous, just as Danny undoubtedly knew it—though Spence didn't think Sadie herself ever had a clue.

She had certainly never flaunted her assets. And at an age when lots of teenage girls were determined to practice their feminine wiles on susceptible males, Sadie had never done that.

If anything, as she'd grown older and more beautiful, she'd got quieter and less forthcoming. As a kid she had always been easy to talk to as she'd tagged around after him and Danny. But by sixteen or so, that had ended. And far from flirting with him whenever he came around with Danny, she became almost distant and remote.

"What'd you do to her?" Danny demanded, seeing her reticence himself and deciding it was because of something Spence had done.

"Nothing! Not a damn thing!"

He'd have spilled blood—even his own—to prove it to Danny. But his protests apparently were enough.

"See that you don't," Danny had said.

"Count on it," Spence had replied. He just figured she didn't like him anymore. As a kid, she'd tagged after him, but as a young woman, she'd evidently seen him for who he was and decided he wasn't worth bothering with.

Better that way, Spence had thought. Better that he not think about Sadie anymore at all.

But then one winter afternoon when he had been in the Morrissey kitchen talking to Danny and tearing his hair over the state of his office and his paperwork, Sadie had walked though, listened a minute, then said, "That's silly. Just file it."

"I would if I could figure out a system!" It wasn't the easiest thing in the world.

"I could figure out a system," Sadie had said blithely, as if she held the answers to all the mysteries in the world.

Spence had snorted. "I doubt it."

"I'll prove it," Sadie had countered.

And the next day she'd shown up at his truck. "So where do you work?"

He'd jerked his head toward the camper top on the truck. "Here."

She'd blinked, then goggled at him, but then shrugged and said. "Fine. Show me."

"You don't want to mess with it," he'd said because he certainly didn't want her poking her nose in his living quarters.

"Afraid I'll be able to do something you can't?" Sadie had challenged.

And of course then he'd had to let her in. So he'd opened the hatch to show her the heaps of paper—notes and scraps and abstracts and legal documents—all tossed around on top of the sleeping bag and mattress he slept on and thrust under the platform where he kept his gear. "Still think you can file it?" He'd given her a lazy smug grin.

"Out of my way." And Sadie had pushed him aside, then clambered in, making him swallow hard as he'd got a good full look at her pert curvy backside disappearing into the back of his truck.

Then she'd turned and looked back at him. "Are you going to help?"

"If I were I'd do it myself," he told her honestly.

She'd nodded. "Then go away."

He had. He'd gone out for a run, determined to wear himself out—and get all thoughts of Sadie's bottom out of his head.

When he came back, exhausted, that evening, he felt more in control of his hormones. Sadie didn't look any more in control of the mess in the back of his truck than she had before he'd left. The paper was still all over the place—in different piles now, but not better piles.

He'd been relieved. And since the next day he had been going to L.A. to a business seminar, he'd said, "Nice try. See. It isn't as easy as you thought. Just forget it."

But Sadie hadn't. She'd shaken her head and held out her hand. "I'm not finished. Give me the key to your truck."

"You're insane." But he'd handed her the key.

When he came back a week later, the mess was gone, the camper was bare except for the platform, mattress, sleeping bag and four filing boxes. He felt a moment's panic.

"Where—?"

"There." Sadie pointed at the filing boxes. "Everything is sorted and in its very own place. I can show you how it works," Sadie had offered.

But the one thing Spence had learned at the seminar was the

value of delegating. He didn't want to know how it worked. He just wanted Sadie there making it work. He'd hired her on the spot.

As his employee, Sadie had stopped being quiet.

She would come every afternoon after school to his truck and sit in the cab, making him go over papers with her, filing them, discussing them, arguing about them. Sadie, for all that she'd been only sixteen, had definite opinions. She'd asked questions about things he'd never even considered.

It wasn't long before he'd realized she wasn't just a genius at organization, she had a good instinctive mind for business—one that complemented his—and he was damned glad she was working for him.

She was gorgeous. She was fun to have around. And she'd become an incredible asset to his work.

The second two he could deal with easily. The first was a problem. Or it would have been if he hadn't learned long ago how to compartmentalize his life.

Dealing with his parents had taught him that. And just as he'd built a "family box" around his parents to keep their anger and bitterness and failure out of his life in order to survive, so he isolated Sadie.

He built a mental "employee box" around her. And then every time he'd found himself even remotely thinking about the physical Sadie Morrissey, he'd slammed the lid on that box.

Until the night Emily had jilted him and the lid had come off. At his rawest, lowest point, Sadie had been there. She'd been gentle, warm, caring, supportive.

Loving.

A word—an experience, let's face it—that Spence knew damn little about. And he'd given in to it. He'd needed her warmth, her care, her love that night. He'd needed Sadie. And he hadn't been able to resist that need.

And so he'd asked her to marry him. Asked? How about

coerced? That was closer to the truth. He'd resisted temptation for years. Had resisted Sadie for years. But that one brief night he had succumbed.

He'd married her. He'd made love to her. He'd—God help him!—taken her innocence that night. At the time he'd been shocked and, perversely, delighted. And of course, faced with her beautiful sleeping face in the morning, he'd known what he'd done was wrong.

Then he'd done what he thought was right—divorced her. Or tried to. Even that, it seemed, he'd done badly. The only thing he'd done right was to stuff Sadie and all his intimate memories of her back into that box and slam the lid on. In the past four years he had never once let himself contemplate her big green eyes or her lovely golden freckled skin or her long long legs or supremely kissable mouth. He had resisted all thoughts of the night he had made love to Sadie Morrissey.

And he sure as hell wasn't going to get through a week of sharing a *bure* at Nanumi with her if he was fixating already on what sort of underwear she wore!

The trouble was, now that he knew—and knew that he was still married to her, knew that legally at least he had a right to her—he couldn't get the vision out of his mind. And he couldn't get his mind out of the bathroom where it had gone to watch her strip off her clothes and get in the shower!

The lid hadn't simply come off, the whole damn box he'd put Sadie Morrissey in for years and years—minus that one fateful night—had crumbled to smithereens.

And his imagination, unleashed, was a fearful thing.

"Get a grip," he muttered furiously to himself. "It's Sadie, for God's sake. It's business."

But his mind—and even more important, his body—were busy reminding him that Sadie wasn't only business; she was his wife.

"For a week," he reminded himself. "Only a week."

Or until the contracts were signed and the resort was a done deal. A week. He could build another damn box and jam her back in for a week.

His body begged to differ.

"Hell!" He stalked over to the door of the bathroom and pounded on it. "Sadie!"

The water shut off. "What?"

He squeezed his eyes shut as if that would keep him from visualizing her standing naked and wet in his shower. "What do you want for dinner?"

What if she said, "You?"

Of course she didn't. "Surprise me," she called back through the closed door.

Spence tried not to think about surprises.

And Sadie must have had second thoughts because she suddenly called, "Just get something they don't have in Butte." And then the water went back on again full force.

Spence stood there drawing in ragged breaths and trying to drag his wits back from wherever they had scattered. "Right. Focus," he commanded himself. "Something they don't have in Butte." Shouldn't be hard.

And certainly a lot simpler than trying again not to think about Sadie Morrissey naked in his shower.

Sadie came out of the bathroom, showered and dressed in clean clothes, feeling better—and warier at the same time.

While she'd been showering, she'd tried to pull herself together, to come to terms with what he'd asked her to do, to convince herself that she could do it without making a fool of herself. She knew she had to or die trying.

At the same time she wasn't even sure how she was going to get through dinner.

Spence was in the kitchen setting out containers on the table.

"It's Burmese," he said. He didn't even look her way, just unloaded white cardboard containers of piping-hot food that made her mouth water, then turned to get plates out of the cupboard. He was moving with customary quick efficiency and he didn't sound angry any longer. Was that good?

"Smells wonderful." Sadie smiled, still a little uncertain.

Spence laid out silverware, then added chopsticks from one of the bags, then filled glasses with ice water and set them on the table.

"Do you want wine?" There was an unopened bottle on the countertop.

"No, thanks. I'd fall asleep." She was fresher than she had been, but still feeling the effects of the night on the plane and the stress of the past two days. "You go ahead."

He didn't open the bottle, however. He just nodded toward the chair closest to her. "Sit down. Dig in."

Sadie sat. "It *looks* wonderful, too."

"Usually is." He opened a container of rice and handed it to her. "I eat at this place whenever I'm in New York. There's beef satay and chicken curry and something with pork that I never remember the name of. Prawn salad and some kind of fritters. You won't get it in Butte." He was talking quickly and shoveling food onto his plate as he did. He still wasn't looking at her.

She dished up some of everything, then picked up her chopsticks. She took a careful breath, then let it out again. Things felt almost…normal. Like the business lunches she and Spence often shared. Only those were accompanied by sheaves of paper, contracts, diagrams, and nonstop talking.

This meal had no paper, no contracts, no diagrams and, right now, no talking. What it had was a big fat determinedly unacknowledged elephant in the room.

The "marriage" elephant. *Their* marriage elephant.

And how it was going to work. Clearly he saw this as a

business effort. But ordinarily when they worked on a project and had agreed on what needed to be done, they sat down and strategized how to do it. They divided up the tasks. They worked out how to support each other. They each had their jobs, and they knew what to expect.

Sadie needed to know what to expect.

But Spence didn't tell her. He didn't say a word. Kept his mouth full or was busy chewing all the time. The whole meal passed in silence. They ate doggedly, determinedly. Until finally there was nothing else to eat. The cartons were empty. Their plates were clean.

And then, when she hoped he might finally speak, he jumped up and began clearing the table.

Sadie stood, too. "Let me help."

"No. It's all right. I'll do it. Kitchen's pretty small." And it was clear he didn't want her anywhere in it. "Coffee? Tea?" He had his back to her again, rinsing off plates in the sink. Since when had Spence become so determinedly domestic?

"Tea, then, please." The cup would give her something to hang on to when at last they came to grips with things. And coffee, she was afraid, would make her already-frayed nerves even more so.

"Okay. Go sit down. I'll get it."

She would have liked to offer to help with that, too. But Spence was already filling the kettle with water and it didn't take two to make tea. So Sadie crossed the room to where she could look out over the back gardens of the block of brownstones.

It was a clear spring evening, already gone dark. And even with the window closed, because it wasn't warm enough yet to leave them open, she could hear the sounds of the city, although muted a bit now. The trees were just coming into leaf. One neighbor's window box was filled with bobbing heads of something that she expected would, in daylight, turn out to be daffodils.

Her own daffodils growing against the wall behind her house back in Butte weren't blooming yet. It was still too cold in Montana. But Montana in the winter felt warmer than this room.

All right. Enough. If he wouldn't bring it up, she would. She turned to where Spence was pouring out cups of tea. "You said it was business, marrying Dena. But you could have married Dena anytime. Why now? What's going on at Nanumi that you need a wife for?"

"You said it yourself. Isogawa wants couples."

"But he wouldn't expect you to marry just to please him. So what else?"

Spence scowled, and Sadie actually thought he wasn't going to answer. But finally, after a long moment, he said, "Leonie."

Sadie blinked. "Leonie? Carstairs?" She didn't follow. "Richard's wife? I don't understand."

Spence's scowl deepened, and something that might have been a tide of red seemed to creep up to his jaw. But he didn't speak as he carried a mug across the room and handed it to her wordlessly.

"Thanks." Sadie accepted it and took a sip, then asked, because she still didn't get it. "Why on earth would you marry Dena because of Richard Carstairs's wife?

"Oh, use your head!" Spence snapped. "Because she doesn't put much stock in being Richard's wife!"

"Doesn't…?" Sadie's voice trailed off. "What?" She considered the implications of what Spence was saying. "You mean…but she's so nice on the phone!"

A harsh breath hissed between Spence's teeth. "How the hell many times has she called you?"

"Three or four. She seems very…nervous. Like she's not sure she's welcome. Not wanting to get in the way."

"Yeah, right," Spence muttered. He hunched his shoulders, looking hunted.

"What's that mean?" Sadie asked. Mentally she ran through the conversations she'd had with Leonie Carstairs. The other woman had seemed perhaps a little overly bright and bubbly when they'd talked, but sometimes a little wistful, too. Richard was always so busy, she'd said. She never knew what she should do.

"She seemed very concerned about whether her husband would have time for her."

"Her husband?" Spence's tone was suspicious.

"Who else?"

He didn't answer, but the fierce red along his jawline and up into his face answered the question for her.

"*You?* You think she's after you?" Sadie gaped at Spence.

"I don't think!" he snarled, dark eyes flashing angrily.

Sadie's eyes widened as she considered the implications. "What's going on?" she finally asked, hoping that inviting him to simply spell it out would get the answers she was missing.

"Leonie Carstairs is a desperate, pushy little tart! A guy is single, she hits on him!"

"She hit…on you?"

"She did." The answer was flat.

"But she's married."

"How naive are you?"

"Oh." Sadie felt her cheeks warm. "Um, I see. But…isn't marrying Dena a little drastic just to get her to stop? Couldn't you just say no?"

"No, damn it, I couldn't!" Spence smacked his mug down on the counter with more force than was necessary, slopping tea everywhere. "I tried that," he added grimly.

Sadie tried not to look agog with interest, just matter-of-fact. But she couldn't help saying, "What happened?" with far more curiosity than she'd intended.

Spence scowled and raked a hand through his hair. "It's a

mess. I've been doing business with Richard for years. Knew his first wife."

"Margaret. Yes, I remember her." While she'd never met either Margaret or Richard Carstairs, she'd enjoyed conversations with them during Spence's dealings with them. And she remembered well when Margaret died five years ago.

"They were perfect together. And then three years ago Richard met Leonie." Spence shook his head. "She's young. He's in his fifties. Hell, his kids are her age! But he wouldn't see reason. He wanted her, and he married her. And now—now it's a hell of a mess." Spence prowled the room like a trapped jungle cat, then flung himself into one of the chairs and looked up at her from beneath hooded lids.

Sadie waited, knowing there were times to prompt Spence and times not to. This was one when she needed to wait him out.

"Now that he's got her, he…doesn't pay a lot of attention to her. Frankly I think she scares him. She scares the hell out of me! She…flirts. To get his attention, I think. At least I thought. Now I don't know. After Barcelona…" He scowled and abruptly stopped talking.

Well, there were some things you couldn't just wait out.

"What about Barcelona?" Sadie demanded. She knew Spence had gone there last month for a meeting. She was the one who'd set it up. And she remembered now that Richard had been scheduled to be there, too. "Leonie was there?" She hadn't scheduled that.

"She was," Spence agreed. "Insisted on coming along, Richard said. But he couldn't take her to all his meetings. So one night she was on her own at the hotel. I didn't pay much attention. It wasn't anything to do with me. I was working. And then, that night, I played poker with some of the guys. Later, when I went back to my room—" he grimaced "—she was in my bed."

Sadie stared. *"In your bed?"*

"You heard me!"

"She was in your *room?* But how…?"

Spence shrugged. "Pretended it was hers. Told a maid she got locked out. She was giggling. Bragging about it. 'A few pesetas is all it takes,' she told me. She thought it was great fun. And she was intent on having more fun. She was—" he rubbed a hand against the back of his neck "—not inclined to take no for an answer."

Sadie felt her mouth go dry. Was he saying he'd slept with Leonie Carstairs?

"I packed her right back out, protesting all the way," Spence answered the question she couldn't ask. "But she wasn't happy about it. 'He'll never know,' she said. 'And if he did find out he wouldn't care.'" Spence shook his head grimly. "Not true. Richard would have damned sure cared. He might leave her for a few hours—she might drive him mad—but as far as he's concerned, she belongs to him. It would have killed our working together. It would have ruined that project. But beyond that, I don't sleep with other men's wives."

Sadie swallowed a surge of relief. "Of course not," she said, happier than she had any right to be.

"When the Nanumi deal came up, I could see Barcelona happening all over again."

"You don't think she got the message?"

"No. She doesn't hear what she doesn't want to hear. But I remembered she tried to hit on Dan Fitzsimmons a few months ago, and then he got married and that was the end of it. She apparently doesn't respect her own wedding ring, but she doesn't poach on other women's husbands."

"So you decided to get married?"

"It sounded like a good idea," he said tersely. "I know you think marriage is all about love and romance and flowers and whatnot, but it's not." He bounded out of the chair and began pacing again. "Marriage, throughout history, has more often been an economic alliance than a hearts-and-flowers romance. I understand that. So did Dena. It would have worked." He turned and faced her, his look challenging her to deny it.

"It still seems…pretty drastic."

"Yeah, well, if you were trying to pull off a several-hundred-million-dollar deal that could be scotched by some floozy with boobs for brains, you might do something drastic, too!"

"And now?"

"Now," he said heavily, "there's you."

Right. The marriage elephant. Front and center.

"So, what are we going to do?" she asked.

"Show up and act like a married couple. In front of everyone else," he qualified quickly. "I don't expect anything else. Don't worry."

Yeah, Sadie had pretty much figured that. But then their gazes met and, for one brief instant, she didn't think that at all. Something vivid and intense and extremely personal seemed to flicker in Spencer Tyack's eyes. Something hot. But before she could be sure, he jerked his gaze away again.

"Come on," he said abruptly. "I'll take you to your hotel."

"Hotel?" Sadie said stupidly, still feeling singed by that momentary heat.

"Hotel. Got you a room at the Plaza. Told you I would, remember?" He was already on his knees, stuffing her pile of dirty clothes into her suitcase and zipping it up as if he couldn't wait to be rid of her.

"I—yes. But I thought that was supposed to be a treat for my having brought your birth certificate and our…divorce papers. I didn't," she added, though she supposed she didn't need to remind him of that.

"Doesn't matter. You've got to sleep somewhere. It's paid for. No sense in it going to waste. Come on." He picked up the suitcase, opened the door and stood there, waiting for her to precede him down the stairs.

And Sadie could hardly say, *I want to stay here*. Could she? No. Of course not.

But the scarier question was: Did she? Was she fool enough to want that?

And if she was honest, then yes, a perverse part—an exceedingly stupid part—of her wanted just that.

But clearly Spence didn't.

He didn't want her. He didn't want to be married to her. And whatever he might have said one night four years ago— those hungry, desperate words he'd murmured that had given her hope that night that she meant more to him than he'd ever let on—had obviously been an aberration, not a heartfelt desire.

Now she sucked in a breath, shoved away all romantic notions of happily ever after, and said what she needed to say. "Very well. Thank you. I'm sure I'll enjoy it." Then, chin held high, she went out the door and down the stairs.

She thought she'd be rid of him then. She'd expected he would hail her a cab and she could crawl into it and stop trying to pretend it didn't matter, that she was indifferent, that she didn't care.

But he didn't just see her into a cab. He got in with her. He accompanied her all the way to the Plaza, where she thought he'd leave her at the door.

But, damn it, he came in with her there. He took care of her registration and then walked her to her room.

"You don't need to," she said desperately.

"I do," Spence said. And she wondered if he heard any irony in his words. Probably not, judging from the studied determination on his face.

She wasn't used to a studiedly determined Spence. She was used to a quicksilver man, a brash, outspoken, clever, wild man. Proper and polite had never been Spence's way—not, at least, around her.

But he was proper and polite tonight. He acted like someone had shoved a copy of Emily Post right up his back.

Go away! she begged him silently. *It's settled. We'll do it. But I need some space. I need some time. I need to be alone.*

The last thing she needed was Spence acting all stiff and solicitous, like this was a duty he was performing—which, of course, it was. It was far worse than being treated in the offhand, breezy way he ordinarily treated her.

At least then it had felt as if they were actually friends. Now that they were still married, there was this terrible tension. It felt awful. Neither of them spoke all the way up in the elevator. He didn't look at her. She didn't look at him.

When they reached her room, he took the key and opened the door for her, then held it so she could precede him. Very stiff, very proper. She felt like kicking him.

The room was big and beautifully decorated and it must have cost him a fortune, not that money was an issue to Spence anymore. He barely seemed to notice the room at all. He'd put her suitcase on the luggage rack, then backed toward the door. There he stopped and looked at her intently. "Are you going to be…all right?"

And what would he do if she said no?

Sadie didn't want to find out. "Why shouldn't I be?" she snapped.

He grimaced. "No reason. It's just…I know it's as awkward for you as it is for me. I'm sorry. About everything and—"

"Well, you don't have to keep going on about it!" She had reached the end of her rope. "Just go!"

"I'm going," he said. "I'll be back in the morning to take you to the airport."

"Don't bother. It's entirely unnecessary, and I can certainly get to the airport by myself." Sadie was grateful that her voice sounded cool and composed. She felt like screaming. "I'll want to get an early flight. That way I can be back home by noon. I have work to do."

He looked almost relieved, as if he could hardly wait for her to be out of the city. "I've got to work in the city all week. I won't have time to get back to Butte before we head out to Fiji."

"I know."

"Right. So get yourself a ticket on my flight to Fiji and I'll see you in L.A. The charter from Fiji won't be a problem. I'll let them know you're coming." He started out the door, then stopped in the hallway. "I just thought…can you get someone to cover while we're gone?"

Cover the office, he meant. They were never both gone at the same time. Or they never had been before. Except once. In Vegas four years ago.

Sadie met his gaze. "I can get someone. Don't worry. Thank you for seeing me here. I won't keep you."

"They have to be competent. No air heads," he went on as if she hadn't spoken.

"I know that." Did he think she was an idiot? "I'll take care of it." *Just go, damn it!*

"Good." There was another pause. He shifted awkwardly. "Thanks." Then he cleared his throat. "I meant what I said earlier, Sadie. You don't have to quit."

That's what all this hemming and hawing was about? He was stalling until he found a way to work that into the conversation.

"It can be like before. We can just go back to—"

"Good night, Spence," she said abruptly.

And she shut the door in his face.

CHAPTER FOUR

IN HER FANTASIES Sadie had spent nights at the Plaza. It was what came of being a bookish child, one who spent hours in the library and who read every single book in the children's section over and over.

She'd loved *Eloise*. She'd read the story of the little girl who lived in the Plaza Hotel until the book cover nearly fell off. To Sadie the Plaza had always seemed more distant than the craters of the moon. She could see the craters of the moon from Butte, Montana. She could only imagine the Plaza.

And now here she was. In her very own room—one that Eloise would have enjoyed immensely. She'd have bounced on the bed and hung by her knees from the shower curtain rod. She'd have rung up room service and ordered whatever she wanted.

Sadie could do that. Spence had said so.

"You didn't eat much at dinner," he'd said when he'd been standing at the registration counter with her. "If you get hungry, order room service. Get whatever you want."

Very magnanimous. Thoughtful. Very proper. A good boss.

Not much of a husband. But then he didn't intend to be.

It shouldn't bother her. She should have got over Spencer Tyack years ago. In fact, she rather thought she had. She had dated other men in the past four years, hadn't she? Just because she hadn't found the right one didn't mean she wasn't looking.

But yesterday, the minute she'd discovered she was still married to him, her world had turned upside down—and all those old desperate completely unreciprocated feelings came right back.

And she couldn't help thinking that, while his wedding with Dena might have been no more than taking their "business" relationship to a new level, no doubt he had planned to spend a wedding night with his new bride. He certainly would not have married her, then packed her off to a hotel by herself while he went back to his apartment alone!

But he'd packed Sadie off to a hotel. He'd acted like he could hardly wait to get rid of her!

She shouldn't be surprised, of course. In fact she wasn't. But it would be so much simpler if she didn't love him, if she never had loved him, if she could just smile carelessly and walk away.

But she couldn't walk away for another week. He wouldn't let her. She sat in the middle of her big bed in the Plaza and felt like crying.

At the same time, she emphatically did *not* want to cry!

She had far more important things to do—like figuring how on earth she was going to survive next week knowing that she wasn't pretending—that she was, in fact, Spencer Tyack's wife.

Wedding nights, according to everything Spence had heard, were supposed to be memorable.

Theo Savas, whose wife, Martha, had painted the murals in Spence's office building, hadn't been able to stop grinning when he'd mentioned his. He'd been completely discreet, of course. Theo would be. But you only had to look at the guy to know that he and his wife had had a very satisfactory time, even though Martha had been in the last stages of pregnancy by the time Theo finally got her to wear his ring.

Lucky Theo, Spence thought grimly.

He could have told Theo a thing or two about memorable wedding nights! He'd had more than his share.

It was mortifying. Humiliating. First Emily's defection four years ago. Then his desperate marriage to Sadie.

And now this! He hadn't had a wedding today—but apparently he still had a wife!

He had tried so scrupulously for four years to forget that night—to forget holding Sadie in his arms, to forget making love to her—that to be hit again with the memories was like being gut-punched.

He might have been all right if he hadn't seen those wispy underthings. When the hell had Sadie started wearing sexy underwear like that?

What he remembered had been cotton and serviceable. Nothing that would stir a guy's libido. Of course, she could have been wearing a gunny sack and it wouldn't have mattered. Once he'd got her out of her clothes, it was all about Sadie.

And his libido had taken over completely.

It had been hard work to walk away from that night—to know that forgetting it was the best thing to do, the only thing to do to be fair to Sadie.

And now it was like all his efforts were for naught.

Why in hell had he had to see those flimsy lacy panties when she'd taken them out of her suitcase? Why couldn't he have been left to contemplate having gone to bed with a Sadie with no more "come hither" attraction than a nun?

Trouble was, he knew Sadie was no nun. Now that he couldn't seem to help but think about that night again, he remembered very well how un-nunlike she had been. Shocked him, really.

She'd always seemed sort of buttoned-down and demure in the office. Well, not demure exactly. But he hadn't counted on a woman who could make his blood run thick and hot.

He'd got one. And so he lay there in his wide lonely bed, twisting and turning, hard and aching—remembering his wedding night!

And, worse, thinking about what it would be like to have Sadie here now—a Sadie in silk and lace. And worst of all, thinking about taking the silk and lace off her. Thinking about running his hands up those long, smooth legs and tugging the scrap of silk down and tossing it aside. Thinking about unfastening that wisp of lace she would call a bra, and letting his hands learn the curve of her breasts, letting his mouth feast on rosy peaks and tease nipples with his tongue.

"Damn it!" He shot out of bed and began pacing the room, his body protesting because walking was *not* what it wanted to do right now. What it wanted was release. Inside warm, wet, willing…Sadie.

Damn it, yes, he remembered!

After years of neatly sticking her in her employee box, her announcement that they were still married had blown the lid right off. It boggled his mind.

He didn't think things like this, or hadn't since he was a hormone-fueled teen. He certainly didn't *do* things like this! He was logical. Sensible. He'd been going to marry Dena, hadn't he?

He was passionate about his work. *Not* about women.

He tried to think. To understand. Was this sudden preoccupation with Sadie because he couldn't have Dena tonight?

It seemed likely. He'd been expecting to have sex with her, and now he couldn't. Even though he admittedly wasn't in love with her, he didn't need love to enjoy a night in bed with a willing woman. He would have enjoyed it.

Enjoyed it a hell of a lot more than he was enjoying this!

He prowled the length of the apartment. It wasn't really big enough for much pacing. But Spence frankly doubted if all of Manhattan was big enough for the pacing he needed to do tonight.

He flicked open the blinds and stood glaring out into the darkness. There were a few lights in other windows. A few others were up at 3:00 a.m. New York never slept.

But he bet Sadie was asleep.

She'd practically nodded off during dinner. She'd sat there with her head bent over her plate, not saying a word. Totally not like Sadie. He was used to her talking his arm off. Tonight he'd got nothing. She couldn't even look at him!

He flung himself down on the bed again and sprawled, staring at the ceiling. Then he rolled over and punched his pillow and kicked the duvet into a heap. It didn't help. He was wired. Strung out.

Sex would help. It would ease his frustration. Relax him.

If Dena were here—

But it wasn't Dena he imagined having sex with! It was a lissome dark-haired woman in peach-colored lace he could see writhing beneath him. It was the same woman he could imagine straddling his thighs, running her hands over his chest, settling lower, taking him in.

"Hell." Spence dragged the pillow over his face. He flung it aside and got up again, then stalked into the bathroom and turned on the cold tap in the shower full blast. Then he stripped off his shorts and stood underneath it, let the frigid water course down his overheated body and cool his ardor.

He stood there until his teeth chattered, until there were goose bumps all over his body. Until he couldn't stand it any longer. Then he got out, dried off and went back to his bed.

And the first thing he thought was that Sadie had been damn lucky he'd been gentleman enough to take her over to the Plaza instead of making her spend the night with him. If he had, he could have peeled those tailored black slacks off her, pulled that burgundy sweater over her head and found the peach-colored tease she wore beneath them.

And damn it to hell, the shower had been useless. Here he was back thinking about Sadie's damn underwear again!

There was a bottle of scotch on the fireplace mantel. It promised solace, consolation. Oblivion. He got up and poured himself a glass, then sat down and stared at it. The fumes tempted him, teased him. Promised him forgetfulness. He'd used it before, right after he'd got the divorce. Or thought he had.

He'd needed to forget. And so he had—until one morning when he actually couldn't remember the night before and it had scared him spitless that he was, exactly as his mother had claimed, just like his old man.

Not that John Tyack had wedding nights he couldn't remember. But the old man had sure as hell had spent plenty of other nights in drunken oblivion. Nights that Spence remembered—and hated—all too well.

He'd stopped drinking right then. He only drank after that if he drank in company, and then only a little. Now, tempted as he was, he turned away from the scotch in disgust and flung himself into the armchair and willed himself to calm down, to cool off, get a grip.

He wasn't his old man. He could find another way out of his pain. Surely he could find another way to forget Sadie and the promise of peach-colored silk.

Of course he could. He had plenty of time. He had the whole rest of the night.

"Are you okay?" Martha Savas poked her head into Sadie's Butte office the next afternoon, frowning and giving her a quizzical, slightly worried glance.

"What? Oh, yes, of course I am." Sadie jerked her brain back to the present and tried to paste a cheerful smile on her face. "Why wouldn't I be?"

"You tell me." And instead of waggling her fingers and

heading down the hall to her studio where she was painting gigantic panels to be hung in a recently renovated bank, Martha marched into Sadie's office and settled into Spence's chair. "You look awful."

"Thank you very much." Sadie kept her tone light, even as she shoved a hand through her hair in an effort to make it look better. But she knew she couldn't do much about the circles under her eyes and the lack of color in her cheeks. "I'm just tired."

"When did you get back?"

"Yesterday afternoon. And I leave again tomorrow."

"Leave? Again? Twice in one week?"

Everyone knew that Sadie never went anywhere. She could get away with explaining that Spence wanted her in New York for a meeting one time. But twice in one week was unheard of.

Martha grinned. "Don't tell me you're finally going to take a vacation."

It was tempting to say she was. After all, a trip to Fiji could be called a vacation, couldn't it?

But she didn't want to lie to Martha. Sadie liked all the artists who had studios or showed their work in the gallery downstairs or the co-op on the second floor, but she liked Martha the most.

When she'd first met Martha, a muralist who had come to Butte just last year, Sadie had felt mortifying twinges of jealousy. After all, Martha had only come because she'd met Spence on a plane coming back from Greece and in his cheerful offhand way, he'd said she ought to come paint a mural for him.

Whether he'd actually ever thought she would or not, Sadie didn't know. But he'd been delighted to see Martha when she'd shown up a few weeks later. And he'd told Sadie to help her find a place to live and suggest places she might look for a job.

"Seattle," Sadie had suggested when she and Martha were alone.

Martha had laughed. "Don't worry. I'm not interested in Spence," she'd said, though Sadie had never once implied she had any interest in Spence, either. She remembered saying so vehemently.

"You don't have to say so." Martha had shrugged. "I'm not blind."

Was it obvious, then? The panic must have shown on her face because Martha had smiled sympathetically and shaken her head. "I see it because I feel the same way—about someone else."

About Theo, it turned out—the man who was now Martha's husband.

But it hadn't been all smooth sailing. When Theo Savas had turned up, determined to marry her, Sadie had watched the drama unfold, enchanted by Martha's tough Greek sailor.

But even though Martha loved him, Theo hadn't had an easy time convincing her to marry him.

"He's being responsible." Martha had dismissed Theo's determined pursuit. "He thinks because I'm pregnant, he needs to marry me."

Well, yes. That had been a complication. And Martha hadn't wanted Theo to marry her out of duty. She'd wanted love.

Sadie understood that feeling. Shared it. Had for years wanted Spence's love. And didn't stand a prayer.

"It's not vacation," she said slowly. "It's…I'm going with Spence to Nanumi—you know, that resort in Fiji—for a week."

Martha's eyes lit up. "Well, hallelujah! He's finally seen the light." She was grinning broadly. "And I didn't even have to hit him over the head with a frying pan." She was absolutely gleeful, and Sadie hated to spoil her good cheer.

"It's…business," she said.

"Oh, right. Business? No. If it were business you'd be here. You're the home front and Spence is the traveling circus."

Sadie wouldn't have put it quite that way, but she understood

Martha's view. "Ordinarily, yes," she agreed. "But this time I get to go, too."

"And not because he's finally interested? He's taking you to a private resort—" Martha invested the words with oodles of innuendo "—to make you work?" She shook her head again. "He's in love."

"He's not. He just…needs a wife."

The minute the words were out, she would have called them back. But it was too late. Martha was staring at her, aghast.

"You're not! Have you lost your mind, Sadie? How manipulative can he be? You are not going to let that bloody man pass you off as his wife!"

Sadie swallowed. "He's not."

"Well, then…" Martha frowned, confused.

"It's true." Sadie shrugged. "I am his wife."

Martha looked as if she'd choked on her tongue. Her mouth opened, but nothing came out. Then she snapped it shut, her eyes still wide and unblinking, and profoundly disbelieving, which had the effect of making Sadie feel about two inches high.

And then quite suddenly Martha's whole expression changed. Her outrage softened. Her features gentled. And she reached for Sadie's hand and squeezed it between her fingers. "For how long?"

Sadie swallowed. "Four years."

She expected Martha to yelp in astonishment. But Martha only sighed and squeezed her hand again. "Oh, you poor dear girl."

The other woman's acceptance and sympathy were very nearly Sadie's undoing. She gulped against the lump in her throat. "It's…my own fault."

"Oh, I doubt that," Martha said dryly. "I know Spence. He can manipulate with the best of them."

"He…well, yes, he can," Sadie admitted. "But he didn't. I mean, he didn't intend to. It's just—"

And then Sadie had to explain. Not all of it. The bare

minimum. She knew Spence would hate her dragging up the past and talking about Emily's jilting him. But in order to make sense of what had happened, Sadie roughed out the general sequence of events, ending with, "He said, 'You'd marry me, wouldn't you?' And, I should have said no."

"I'd like to know how," Martha said tartly. "When Spence gets a notion, he doesn't back off. He's like a bulldozer. Besides—" her tone softened "—you loved him."

"But he didn't love me!" Sadie protested. "You wouldn't marry Theo when you thought he didn't love you!"

"That was different," Martha said. "I didn't know Theo. Not really. We hadn't known each other for years like you and Spence. We'd had a fling. And that was my fault, not his."

Sadie stared at her. "Your fault?"

"Long story," Martha said with a wry smile. "Suffice to say I was the one who pushed Theo into the fling. No strings, I said. Just mind-blowing sex—" She reddened. "Stop looking at me like that. I was crazy, all right? Anyway, he agreed. So I knew he only wanted an affair. So when he turned up demanding to marry me after I got pregnant, I certainly didn't think it was because he was in love with me."

"But he was," Sadie said with satisfaction, remembering Theo's determined courtship, his last desperate gesture. "It was so romantic."

"It was insane," Martha said.

"But he convinced you. You knew he loved you then. And so you married him. Not like me. I married Spence because I thought…I hoped…"

But she couldn't even bring herself to voice those desperate hopes. Instead she blinked furiously, hating the tears that welled up in her eyes. "Because I'm an idiot," she muttered.

"He's the idiot," Martha said without hesitation. She crossed one leg over the other knee. "So what happened?"

"He was going to marry Dena Wilson. He wanted me to bring him his birth certificate and the divorce papers. He called, told me, then hung up. And I went looking where he told me to look—and he hadn't got them. He thought he had and tossed the envelope in the file. But it was a preliminary letter, not even close to a decree. And I couldn't reach him because he never turns his phone on. So I had to go to New York…and tell him."

"What? At the wedding?" Martha grinned when Sadie nodded. "Well, that will teach him to keep his phone on!"

Sadie grimaced. "I guess. And we will get a divorce, but we can't yet. He…needs a wife in Fiji this coming week."

"Needs a wife?"

"It's business," Sadie said firmly. "And perfectly legitimate. He's just making the best of a bad situation."

"Did he *say* that?"

"Not precisely."

"Lucky for him. I'd have killed him if he had," Martha said bluntly. She sighed. "This is difficult."

"I know," Sadie agreed. "But I have to do it."

"Why?"

Confronted with the question that bluntly, Sadie couldn't find the words. Finally she mumbled something about owing him.

"You don't owe him a damn thing," Martha said indignantly.

"I agreed to marry him. And I'm still…his wife." Sadie actually managed to get the words out. "I can do this," she said in the face of Martha's doubt. "It will be all right. Then we can divorce. And…and I can walk away."

"Oh, for heaven's sake!" Martha stared at her. "Are you listening to yourself? You *love* him. How can you walk away?"

Sadie knew better than to deny it. "You walked away from Theo."

"Actually, I didn't. Theo left me."

"What?" Sadie stared in astonishment.

"He left Santorini and went to the States. And then I left, too, because it hurt so much to be there without him. And maybe that's when I was really an idiot, because before I was due to go home, he came back."

Sadie's eyes widened further. "Really?" She wanted to hear more. It was far better to hear a story with a happy ending than to contemplate her own miserable one.

But Martha said, "What happened between Theo and me doesn't matter here. What matters is that if you love Spence and have loved him for years—not to mention having spent *four years* married to him!—you can't just walk away. You have to fight for him."

Sadie stared at her.

"You do," Martha said. "Unless you're giving up. And frankly, I never thought you were a quitter." The words dripped challenge.

But Sadie resisted. "And how am I supposed to do that? Arm wrestle him? If I win, he has to stay married to me? No, thanks. Besides—"she sighed "—I wouldn't win."

"So, you're going to give up? Just go for a week in paradise with the man you love, and then turn tail and run?"

"It isn't what I *want* to do!" Sadie protested, realizing the truth even as she said it. "But it's not going to work! I've known him forever, I've worked for him for years, and he's never *ever* even asked me out!"

"But he asked you to marry him," Martha reminded her. "And not for business. Think about that."

Sadie did. She thought about something else, too—the one thing that had kept her hopes up all these years. She thought about what had happened on their wedding night when they'd come back to the honeymoon suite where he'd intended to bring Emily.

Sadie had been wary and worried, waiting for Spence to come to grips with the realization that he had married the wrong woman.

But Spence had been completely intent on her. They'd barely got in the door when he'd kissed her deeply, passionately, with all the fervor of a man in love.

Sadie had been stunned—and delighted. And she'd responded with all the eagerness she'd held in her heart for so long. She'd returned the kiss, had deepened it, had pulled his shirt out of his trousers and run her hands over his heated skin. She'd encouraged him when he'd moved to pull her top over her head. She'd leaned into his hungry embrace, ravenous herself.

And when he'd taken her to bed, she'd gone willingly, eagerly, as desperate for him as he'd been for her—even though she feared he was pretending she was Emily all the while.

Their lovemaking had been fast and frantic and delicious. It had ended with them clinging to each other, shattered and spent.

And then Spence had drawn her tight against him and whispered raggedly, "It always should have been you."

She thought about that now. Had he meant it? Had he even known he'd said it? He'd certainly never said it again, nor anything remotely like it. But still, if he had…

"You're very quiet," Martha said now.

"Just…thinking."

"Finding a reason to fight?" Martha speculated.

Sadie ventured a tentative smile. "Maybe so."

He didn't call Sadie the rest of the week.

Why should he? She'd be in L.A. on Friday. They'd have hours on the plane to catch up on work. He didn't need to talk to her every day, even though it was a rare day he didn't. Or used to be a rare day. Now it wasn't that important. She knew her job. She was clever. She was competent.

She was his wife.

And Spencer Tyack didn't have a clue what to say to a wife. Not a wife who was Sadie, at least.

If he had married Dena, talking would have been no problem at all. They could have discussed work, upcoming projects they might pursue, the logistics of the resort financing.

Of course he'd always talked about business with Sadie, too. Often. But not now. Not when he kept remembering her peach-colored silk. Not when his tongue seemed welded to the roof of his mouth. Not when his memories of the night they'd spent together all crowded back into his brain and wouldn't let him think of anything else.

That Sadie he couldn't talk to at all!

Which didn't matter, of course, because she had never rung him, either. Not once.

She'd never called to say she got home. Had never updated him on any of their current projects—not that there were any in immediate need of his attention—but she might at least have let him know the status of things. She'd never even called to tell him when her flight to L.A. was arriving.

Their only communication all week was when he'd sent her an e-mail or a text message telling her what he needed her to do.

Far more efficient than phone calls, he assured himself. They should have been doing this for years. But that was infuriating, too, because the only response he ever got was the single-word reply, "Done."

He'd sent her five texts today, though, all updating his progress across the country. He never got a reply to those. He'd sent her another as soon as he'd landed in L.A. Again no answer. Of course she might be en route herself.

But he didn't like not knowing.

They were going to have to sort things out as soon as she got here. It damned well wasn't going to work if she ignored him at Nanumi. Mr. Isogawa was sharp. He wasn't going to be convinced that they were a solid stable couple if they snarled at each other or avoided each other the whole week.

And even if Isogawa didn't notice a rift, Leonie undoubtedly would, and there was a good chance she'd try to exploit it.

Spence knew he'd been lucky to get her out of his room in Barcelona without Richard's ever learning that she'd come calling in the first place. And he didn't want the same thing happening again. He liked Richard. He actually even liked Leonie, when she wasn't behaving like a tart. And Richard's millions were an absolute necessity to the resort investment package.

Leonie could destroy that—and her marriage—and that wouldn't be good for anyone.

So no matter whether he and Sadie felt like talking or not, he was going to have to spell out what he expected of his wife. And, God help him, he was going to have to behave like a husband.

"So," a familiar voice said behind him, "I'm here."

Spence spun around at the sound, and yes, she was—right here in front of him: Sadie Morrissey looking exactly the way Sadie Morrissey always did neat, professional, appropriate, in control. Thank God.

And yet, even so, his heart did a weird kick-thump in his chest at the sight of her because his first thought was, what sort of underwear was she wearing?

His eyes screwed shut as his brain tried to get his hormones under control. But did they listen? Not on your life. He steeled himself against his reactions, scowling at how inappropriate they were.

"Obviously you're glad to see me," Sadie said dryly. "Did you change your mind, then?" There was an edge to her voice that said she wasn't any more thrilled than he was.

"What? No, of course not. I'm just relieved you finally got here." He made a point of glancing at his watch. "Cutting a little close, weren't you?"

"Was I? I don't think so. I had things to arrange," she reminded him loftily. "Anyway, I'm here now."

And without another word, she turned, walked straight over to a bank of seats and sat down.

Spence stalked after her, annoyed at what seemed like blatant dismissal, "So you got 'backup'?"

"Of course. I wouldn't be here if I hadn't."

"Who?"

There was a split second's hesitation. Then, "Grace."

"Grace?" He stared at her. "Grace Tredinnick? Have you lost your mind? Grace is eighty if she's a day!"

"Eighty-two, actually," Sadie said, her chin coming up, her gaze steely. "Her birthday was in January. The eleventh. I sent her a card." Subtext: you didn't. "Did you know she graduated from the Butte Business College? She was valedictorian."

"No," Spence said through his teeth. "I damned well didn't know it. And I'll bet you didn't either until yesterday."

"The day before, in fact."

"I don't care if you knew it last month! That doesn't qualify her to run my business. What the hell were you thinking? Tyack's is a multimillion dollar international firm and—"

"—and you insisted that I come with you. And I couldn't answer all the correspondence and deal with the day-to-day stuff from the middle of the Pacific Ocean, so I had to find someone who could. On short notice. I found Grace," she added belligerently.

"Grace can't—"

"Grace certainly can! And in case she wants some help, she won't be doing it alone."

"Oh." He breathed a sigh of relief, still annoyed that she'd just been winding him up to annoy him, but glad she'd got competent help. "Well then—"

"I also found Claire and Jeremy."

"Jeremy!" Now he really was apoplectic. "Claire's all right, I suppose. At least she's not a criminal, though she is about

fifteen. But Jeremy! For God's sake, Sadie! He's a juvenile delinquent!"

"Was. And of course, no one who's ever been a juvenile delinquent could possibly do anything constructive with his life!"

They both knew that Spence had been a far bigger delinquent than Jeremy in his time.

He scowled furiously. "I paid my dues."

"As has Jeremy. He did a fantastic job on the mural and you know it. Besides, Theo and Martha both vouch for him. They think he'll do a terrific job. And you know he won't cross Grace."

"How do I know he won't mug and murder Grace?"

"Because he got sent to juvie for painting graffiti, not for knocking off old ladies! For heaven's sake, Spence! He got an A in bookkeeping last semester. And Claire is in the Future Business Leaders of America."

"Bully for her. Is Grace in the *Past* Business Leaders?"

"I wouldn't know. I do know they'll be fine! And if you don't want them, say so now and I'll turn around and go straight home!"

Her eyes flashed fire, her freckled cheeks were big blotches of red, and she was glaring at him the same way she always did when they were battling it out, and quite suddenly Spence felt a real overwhelming sense of relief. She was still his Sadie after all.

He grinned. And then felt an instant stab of panic as he realized that *his* Sadie might at this very moment be wearing scraps of silk and lace. And was his wife!

His grin vanished. He needed to talk to her about that. But not now. Not when he was beset by a sudden vision of peach-colored underwear. He took a shaky breath. "Well…we'll see, won't we?"

He was talking about Grace, Claire and Jeremy. Really, he was. He was *not* talking about seeing Sadie—his wife!—in her underwear. It didn't even occur to him. Not consciously.

Not then.

* * *

Well, so much for that.

All her hopes and dreams and professed determination to make Spence sit up and take notice and want to stay married to her—the ones that had actually seemed possible when she'd been sitting in Butte, encouraged by Martha—didn't stand a chance.

He was treating her exactly the way he always had. Barking at her, arguing with her. And she was instinctively barking back. Of course she knew that her choice of Grace, Claire and Jeremy would rile him. But she truly hadn't had any choice. Not if she was going to come along. And despite her fretting, the more she thought about it, the more she knew she had to.

As Martha said, she couldn't just walk away without a fight.

But fight over Grace wasn't exactly what she'd had in mind.

"Sorry," she said now as they boarded the plane and settled in spacious business-class seats. "It was the best I could do. And I do think everything will be fine. She does have the number at Nanumi in case there's a problem."

Spence grunted, which she hoped meant he was mollified. She wasn't sure. He had stowed her carry-on in the compartment overhead, but he kept his own briefcase with him and took out a sheaf of papers.

"We need to go over these," he said.

"Now?"

"Of course."

So much for any plans for a heart-to-heart. Obviously in Spence's eyes she had only come along as his wife to play a part.

Sadie ran her tongue over her lips and tried to swallow hard to dislodge the lump of disappointment that seemed to be stuck in her throat. "Fine," she said, with all the equability she could muster. "Let's."

It was back to normal with a vengeance then, as Spence talked nonstop. He seemed to have stored up a week's worth of things to discuss with her, letters he wanted her to write, research he wanted her to do.

While she had spent the last three days gearing herself up for the coming week—trying to imagine how she would deal with life as Spencer Tyack's wife, how she would share a *bure* with him, smile lovingly at him, kiss him—Spence seemed not to have thought about it at all.

"…paying attention, Sadie?"

"What?" Her cheeks reddened as she tried to jerk her mind back to whatever he'd been saying. "I'm sorry. I'm feeling a little cramped. My feet are going to sleep. Maybe if I walked around. I'll be right back."

Spence looked disgruntled, but obligingly folded up the papers and pulled his legs back against his seat so she could slide past his knees to get into the aisle.

At least she had far more room to do so than in coach class. Even so she was acutely conscious of the brush of his knees against the backs of her legs. "Sorry," she murmured. "Back in a minute."

It wasn't a minute. She took her time, walked the aisle, went to the rest room, splashed a little water on her face. When she got back, the flight attendant was just bringing her meal. And after the meal, just as Spence was about to drag out his papers again, the in-flight movie began.

"Oh, good! Hugh Jackman!" Sadie was delighted. And she made more of her delight than was absolutely necessary because, even more than Hugh Jackman, she liked not having to try to deal with Spence for a couple of hours.

"I suppose you want to watch that. Be my guest. I'll get some work done."

And he got out his laptop and began tapping away furiously on it. The film was good. Even so, it took Sadie a while to lose herself in it and not in the mess that was her life. Sometime later, though, she noticed that Spence had stopped typing.

She glanced his way, expecting to see him caught up in the film, too. Instead he was frowning at her.

"Something wrong?" she asked.

He jumped, looking startled, then quickly shook his head. "No." His tone was abrupt, and he immediately went back to his laptop.

Sadie sighed and tried to lose herself in the film again. But all she could do was hear Spence typing furiously next to her. What was that all about?

When the movie ended and the lights came back on again, he stopped typing and looked at her.

"We have to talk." He was looking very dark and grave. Very un-Spencelike.

"All right," Sadie said cautiously.

He didn't, though. Not for a moment. He seemed to be weighing what he was going to say, which was also totally not like Spence. With her, Spence always said the first thing that came into his head and then they argued about it.

"I know why you married me," he said at last.

He knew?

Knew she loved him? Sadie felt her marvelous first-class meal climb into her throat. She clamped her teeth together and prayed it would go right back down again. And she didn't open her mouth until she was sure it had.

Then she said, "Do you?"

She wanted to sink into the earth—a difficult feat at any time but particularly when one was 38,000 feet above it.

He nodded, still dead serious. "And I want you to know I do appreciate it."

Appreciate it? She frowned. What?

She *loved* him and he *appreciated it?*

"I realize now that you were only trying to help," he went on solemnly. "To do what needed to be done, what was best for the company." He leaned toward her earnestly.

She stared at him, stunned. *That* was why he thought she'd married him?

"And I'm very grateful. I know it was hard on you. The marriage. After. And the divorce—well, the nondivorce," he said, his mouth twisting "has only made things worse. But we can make the best of a bad situation. We're adults. Right? Mature, sensible, sane."

Were they? Then why was she feeling like killing him? She didn't say a word, just stared at him.

"We can handle this," he went on. "Can't we?"

He was looking at her expectantly, as if she was supposed to be saying something in response to his comment.

Like what? *I love you, you stupid idiot?* He had no clue.

Spence's expression grew impatient. "Fine. If you don't want to discuss it, we won't. I'm sorry you feel that way. I'm just trying to say I understand. I'm…grateful."

Oh, good, just what she wanted—gratitude!

"I also hope this isn't going to be too difficult for you—what I'm asking you to do," he added stiffly.

"What *are* you asking me to do?" she said, irritated. "Exactly, I mean?"

Might as well get it all spelled out. She was reasonably sure that "loving him forever" wouldn't come up.

At her question, something that might have been a flush climbed into his face. "Nothing compromising," he assured her.

"Compromising? What sort of word is that?" She couldn't stop herself. She'd battled with him too often.

And Spence knew a challenge when he heard it. "You know damn well what sort of word it is! I'm not expecting you to sleep with me!"

Well, she'd asked. *Take that*, Sadie said to herself. "Of course you aren't," she murmured, more to herself than to him.

But he heard her and his gaze narrowed. "I do expect you to act like my wife. My happily married wife."

Deliberately Sadie widened her eyes, goading him. "Which means?"

Spence ground his teeth. "See if you can pretend to like me. Just a little."

"I do like you," Sadie said truthfully. "When you're not acting like an ass."

His brows drew down. "What's that supposed to mean?"

"It means that you trust me to do everything else. Trust me to do this."

He looked momentarily taken aback. Then he nodded jerkily. "Of course. I do. I…just want it clear. So Leonie knows," he added. "And Isogawa."

"They'll know," Sadie promised heavily, suddenly tired.

All her initial determination to make this work was gone. Spence was all about pretending. He didn't want anything real she had to offer.

"Okay, then." Spence let it go for a minute, then added, "You realize we are going to have to share a *bure*, though. One of those thatched cottages. They have a bedroom and a living room. Two beds."

And that was more than Sadie had any desire to discuss right now. Maybe it was because she'd been operating on adrenaline ever since Spence had said he was marrying Dena. Maybe it was because her dreams had suddenly come back to life only to be mocked by Spence's determination to pretend. She didn't know. She just knew she couldn't deal with it—with him!— any longer.

"Right," she said. "Two beds. Fine. Whatever. I will do my best to convince Leonie and Mr. Isogawa and everyone else that

I am a deeply devoted wife. Now, if you're finished explaining my duties, I'd like to go to sleep."

And without giving him a chance to reply, she wrapped herself in the blanket the attendant had given her earlier, reclined the seat as far as it would go, turned her back on him and shut off her light.

CHAPTER FIVE

SADIE slept the whole rest of the flight.

Spence knew that for a fact—because he couldn't.

He tried, God knew. He was used to grabbing forty winks wherever he could—in a bank lobby, on an airplane, standing up in a hallway. A man who'd slept in his truck for two years could sleep anywhere.

Except, apparently, when Sadie Morrissey was sleeping next to him.

He watched her for hours in teeth-grinding frustration, wide-awake, wired and ready to chew glass, while Sadie, having frozen him out when he'd been trying to be understanding, damn it, slept like the proverbial baby.

The trouble was she didn't look like a baby. Babies didn't have tousled dark hair that brushed against their cheekbones. They didn't smile and sigh erotically in their sleep. They didn't twist and turn and flip the blanket away so that bits of bare midriff peeked out.

Spence didn't want to see bits of Sadie's bare midriff. Not if that was all he got to see. He didn't want to feel the temptation to reach over and run his fingers lightly along those few inches of soft, pale skin. Not if he couldn't just hook his fingers right under the edge of her shirt and tug it over her head. Not if he couldn't unzip her slacks and slide them down her endless legs.

"Damn it!" The words hissed through his teeth. He jerked his gaze away and clenched his hands on the armrests of the seat.

"Sir?" The flight attendant appeared at his elbow. "Is everything all right?" She bent down and was peering at him worriedly.

Spence dragged in a harsh breath. "Everything's fine," he said in a low controlled voice. "I just…remembered something."

What it was like to have Sadie naked in his arms!

"Can I get you anything?"

Knockout drops? A stun gun?

"Coffee," he said at last. "Lots of coffee. I need to work."

There was always plenty to be done. And he'd always done it, using work to put his life's circumstances out of his mind. To forget his jerk of a father, to blot out his shrewish mother. He'd used work earlier on the flight, talking about the projects to Sadie because when they talked about work, he had things under control.

The flight attendant brought him coffee. He booted up his laptop again. He opened a file, focused on the specs of the Sao Paulo building Mateus Gonsalves was recommending that they buy.

Tried to focus. It didn't work. He muttered under his breath.

"Mmmm?" Sadie shifted and turned his way.

Swell. Now if he shifted his eyes even slightly he could see her face, feast his gaze on her slightly parted mouth. He had kissed that mouth. Really kissed it. Not just given Sadie the duty peck that he had allowed himself to bestow as a part of their friendship-business relationship.

She had a generous mouth. A kissable mouth. And he was going to have to kiss her again this week. Not just brush his lips over hers but—in the interest of their convincing portrayal of a newly married couple—drown himself in her kiss. And bury himself in—

Stop! Just stop!

Wanting Sadie Morrissey was the last thing he should do.

She didn't want him. She'd married him out of kindness, damn it!

He'd told her he understood why she'd done it—out of care for the company—because the truth was worse. When Emily jilted him, Sadie had felt sorry for him. He'd said gruffly, "You'd marry me. Wouldn't you?" And she had because what the hell else was she supposed to say?

She'd married him out of pity!

The very thought made him cringe. It made him squirm.

He didn't want pity. Never had. He had hated it when the teachers had tsked and murmured about his father, about what a hard life he'd had. Sure, his life might have been easier with different parents, but he'd done fine.

He'd survived, hadn't he? He always would.

He didn't know what the hell she'd got mad about, either. He had only been trying to do her a favor by reassuring her that he didn't intend to jump her bones. He could control himself. He hoped.

Besides they wouldn't be sharing a bed. Only a *bure*. They would be fine.

He glanced her way again, determined to steel himself against the attraction. But there was more midriff showing.

He shut his eyes. Heard her move, then mutter. She flung an arm out and it landed on him. His eyes flew open. Sadie's fingers curved around his forearm, warm and possessive.

They were long and slender fingers with sensible short nails, well-trimmed and neat—just like Sadie. Looking at them a guy would never think they belonged to a woman wearing lacy peach-colored silk. There was nothing particularly sexy or erotic about them—until all of a sudden her thumb began to stroke his sleeve.

At her touch Spence jerked, then looked at her suspiciously. Was she awake? Having him on? Or reading his mind?

But her breathing didn't change. She just smiled. He swallowed and barely breathed, but he didn't move his arm, didn't pull away, because beneath the cotton of his shirt, his skin tingled at her touch.

Once upon a time, four years ago, he remembered burning under Sadie's touch. He shut his eyes and tried not to think about it. He should have had his head examined for insisting she come along.

But it had seemed perfectly sane and sensible at the time, no different than taking Dena.

Ha.

Sadie hadn't expected to sleep. She certainly hadn't expected to be refreshed by it. So she was amazed to wake up to hear the sounds of a breakfast cart rattling nearby and to feel almost human and hopeful again.

She stirred and shifted, keeping her eyes slitted as she turned so she could catch a glimpse of Spence.

He was slouched in his seat, looking stubble-jawed and rumpled, his hair a little spiky, his eyes a little tired as he stared at some papers in his hand. She doubted he had slept at all.

She sighed and stretched and slowly opened her eyes the rest of the way. Spence didn't look up until she sat up and began to fold the blanket. Then he glanced her way.

"Sleep well?" he growled.

"I did, actually," Sadie said. She took a brush out of her purse and ran it through her hair, then fished out a lipstick and a mirror. "Almost human."

Spence grunted and went back to his papers.

When she'd finished to her satisfaction, she straightened and looked over at him. "Did you work the whole flight?"

"I had things to do. Work to catch up on. And I wanted to be prepared." His tone was gruff and he flexed his shoulders as if trying to get a little of the tension out of them.

"You don't think a little sleep might have done more for you?" Sadie said lightly.

"I said I had work to do," he said sharply.

"Sorry," Sadie said lightly. She paused, then decided maybe she'd been a little too abrupt earlier. He couldn't help what he didn't feel.

"I'll do my part," she assured him.

He looked over at her. "What?"

"When we land. I'll do my part. You don't have to worry. I'll…be your wife."

He stared at her a long moment. There was something there in his gaze again when it connected with hers that seemed, to Sadie, almost electric.

Don't, she warned herself. *Do not read anything into this. It's your brain. Your emotions. Your dreams. It's not real.*

And then, "Right," Spence said, and gave her a jerky nod just as the flight attendant appeared with their breakfasts.

They ate. And then after, as the dishes were being removed, the captain announced that they'd begun their descent and they needed to put everything away in preparation for landing.

And suddenly Sadie felt the shiver of nerves all over again. It felt oddly like childhood piano recitals when all of the expectations of her teacher, Sister Catherine Marie, came to rest on her thin shoulders. She trembled briefly.

Spence stood up and put his computer and files away, then rummaged in his carry-on and sat back down again. "Here," he said, almost offhandedly, and a small black velvet box landed in her lap.

Sadie jumped as if it were a grenade.

"It's not going to blow up," Spence said gruffly. "Open it."

OFFICIAL OPINION POLL

ANSWER 3 QUESTIONS AND WE'LL SEND YOU
4 FREE BOOKS AND A FREE GIFT!

0074823 IIII■III■IIII II■■IIII II■IIIII FREE GIFT CLAIM # 3953

YOUR OPINION COUNTS!

Please tick TRUE or FALSE below to express your opinion about the following statements:

Q1 Do you believe in "true love"?

"TRUE LOVE HAPPENS ONLY ONCE IN A LIFETIME."
○ TRUE
○ FALSE

Q2 Do you think marriage has any value in today's world?

"YOU CAN BE TOTALLY COMMITTED TO SOMEONE WITHOUT BEING MARRIED."
○ TRUE
○ FALSE

Q3 What kind of books do you enjoy?

"A GREAT NOVEL MUST HAVE A HAPPY ENDING."
○ TRUE
○ FALSE

YES, I have scratched the area below.

Please send me the 4 FREE BOOKS and FREE GIFT for which I qualify. I understand I am under no obligation to purchase any books, as explained on the back of this card.

P7II

Mrs/Miss/Ms/Mr   Initials

BLOCK CAPITALS PLEASE

Surname

Address

Postcode

Visit us online at www.millsandboon.co.uk

The Reader Service™ — Here's how it works:

Accepting the free books and gift places you under no obligation to buy anything. You may keep the books and gift and return the despatch note marked 'cancel'. If we do not hear from you, about a month later we'll send you 6 additional books and invoice you just £2.89*. That's the complete price – there is no extra charge for postage and packing. You may cancel at any time, but if you choose to continue, every month we'll send you 6 more books, which you may either purchase or return to us - the choice is yours.

NO STAMP
NEEDED!

THE READER SERVICE™
FREE BOOK OFFER
FREEPOST CN81
CROYDON
CR9 3WZ

NO STAMP
NECESSARY
IF POSTED IN
THE U.K. OR N.I.

But Sadie couldn't. She couldn't even pick it up. Her breath seemed caught in her throat. She regarded the box warily, wordlessly.

"Too awful to contemplate?" Spence growled. "Come on, Sadie. You can't be my bride without rings. What are you waiting for? Me to put them on you?"

His rough tone galvanized her voice at least. "Of course not!"

It was just a shock. So…unexpected.

She guessed she shouldn't be surprised. Spence believed in covering all the bases. That's what had made his screw-up of their divorce such a shock. Now she prayed that her fingers wouldn't tremble as she picked up the box and carefully eased open the spring closure.

"It's not booby-trapped, either," Spence said irritably.

"No." She barely breathed the word as the lid opened and she simple stared. Didn't move. Didn't speak.

"You don't like them," Spence said after a moment. His voice was flat. "They aren't exactly…traditional."

No. That was what was so remarkable about them.

Sadie had seen the ring he'd bought Emily—a showy elegant diamond with little rubies all around it. She didn't know what he'd done with it after Emily hadn't shown up. At least, thank God, he hadn't given it to *her*.

She'd glimpsed the engagement ring Dena had worn—a diamond solitaire on a white-gold band. Polished and sophisticated, like the woman who had worn it.

"I suppose I could've just given you Dena's," he said now. "But I didn't think—"

"No," Sadie said, the word torn from the depths of her soul. "No," she said again. "Not those. These." She tipped the box to allow more light in. There were two rings—a thin gold filigree band with an exquisitely cut piece of jade inlaid for an engagement ring. And the wedding ring was pure jade inset into a bead of Celtic knots. Her Morrissey ancestors would have approved. A circle of green and gold fire. Primitive and perfect. Completely her.

"Dena's rings were worth a hell of a lot more, moneywise," he said. "But they didn't…look right. Didn't look like something you'd wear."

Numbly Sadie shook her head. "No. I wouldn't."

If he'd brought Dena's for her to wear, she would have turned the diamond into her palm, clenched her fingers around it and never opened her fist. But it's what she would have expected.

After all, what difference would it have made, if they were only going to be married a week?

These rings, however, were so completely "her" it was spooky. How had Spence known? She shot him a quick probing glance, amazed.

"I didn't buy you one the first time," he reminded her.

"I know. But you gave me that old pipestone ring you used to wear."

He stared at her.

"Don't you remember it? The one that belonged to your granddad."

"My granddad's ring?" He looked stunned. "I thought I'd lost it."

Sadie shook her head. "No. You took it off and gave it to me. Put it on my finger," she told him. "Until you got me something better, you said." She shrugged. He still looked poleaxed by the news. "You really didn't remember?"

He shook his head, looking almost dazed.

"Well, you were gone a month, you know…after. And then I guess I forgot. I should have given it back to you."

The truth was, she hadn't forgotten. And she never would. She'd loved that ring. It was precious to her. And she'd kept it on a chain around her neck for the next month. Only after

Spence had come in and told her the divorce was final had she removed it.

She would have given it to him if he'd asked, but he never had. So she had put it in the drawer of her bedside table. More nights than she liked to remember she opened that drawer right before she went to sleep. She touched the ring and thought about what might have been.

"I still have it." She swallowed, then made herself say words she never wanted to say. "You can have it back if you want."

"I'd…like that." His voice had a ragged edge. "It's the only thing I had that belonged to him. We can trade. If you want," he added quickly. "If you don't like these I can get you something else. I just thought—"

"I *do* like them," Sadie said fervently. "They're…beautiful. Truly. That seems like such an overused word, I know. But they are. They're…perfect." And as she spoke, she reached out a finger and touched them with something almost like reverence. She felt tears well up.

"Good God, you're *not* going to cry!"

That only made her blink even faster. But at least she took a deep quick breath and said, "Of course not. I'm just…I think they're wonderful. Thank you."

"Well, good," he said gruffly. "So, aren't you going to put them on?"

Carefully Sadie took the wedding ring out of the box and slid it onto her finger.

"It might be too big," Spence said.

But it wasn't. It fit perfectly.

"It's the color of your eyes," he said suddenly, surprising her even more. She might have known him for most of her life, but she'd never have imagined he'd know what color her eyes were.

Now she turned them on him and saw that there was a definite flush of red over his cheekbones.

"They're like that forest pool in that kids' book," he told her. And even as he said so, the color got deeper. "The one you made me read you when you were little. That fairy tale." He looked completely embarrassed now.

"I remember that!" When Spence had been in fifth grade she'd talked him into reading her a storybook fairy tale in which there had been a picture of a magical pool like that. Danny wouldn't have been caught dead reading her fairy stories. But Spence had no little sisters pestering him all day, so he'd indulged her. And if he hadn't already, he'd won her heart by telling her that the pool in the forest was the same color as her eyes.

She remembered now that she'd been amazed. "Really? The magic pool? Are my eyes magic?"

"Sure," he'd said then. Now he insisted, "They were that color. It's not like I was making something up."

"No. Of course not!" Sadie grinned. She felt suddenly deliriously happy. She took out the other ring and felt a moment's fleeting temptation to ask Spence to put it on her finger.

But he'd come much further than she'd ever believed he would already. It wouldn't do to push. So she slid it on herself. It, too, fit perfectly.

She lifted her gaze and met his. "Thank you. They're beautiful."

He cleared his throat. "Glad you like 'em. You keep them. After, I mean."

"After?"

"After the week is up," he clarified.

She was still smiling, but it froze on her lips.

"I don't want them back," he went on. "They're for you."

For her? But he was still planning on divorce at the end of the week? She could hear Martha now saying, "I don't *think* so!"

Sadie didn't know what to think.

* * *

The ring thing had shaken him.

Not just the rings he'd bought her, which he was very glad she liked and which suited her—though he couldn't quite make out why she'd blown warm and then very cold right at the end—but even more than Sadie's new rings, what shook him was realizing she had his grandfather's pipestone ring, and that he had given it to her the night they'd wed.

It just proved what a daze he'd been in. He couldn't imagine having given that ring to anyone.

It was big, awkward, homemade. His grandfather's father had carved it out of pipestone he'd found when he'd first come to Montana to mine as a young man. The ring was a heavy dark red inlaid with a piece of mother-of-pearl in the rough shape of a heart.

"He always said he reckoned he'd give the heart to my ma when she got here," his grandfather had told the young Spence. It had taken the young miner three years to save up enough money to bring over the family he'd left behind in Cornwall.

But only the children—a boy and a girl he barely recognized—had got off the train in Butte that summer morning. His wife had died on the voyage.

"So he wore the ring," Grandpa had said. "And the heart."

The red pipestone with its mother-of-pearl heart had stayed on his finger until the day he'd died, though the mother-of-pearl heart had cracked and a chip was missing.

Grandpa had worn it that way, too. "To remember," he'd said.

When he died, it had gone to Spence's dad who had never worn it.

"Don't like rings," he'd always said. He'd never worn a wedding ring either. So the pipestone ring used to sit in the saucer on top of his bureau. Spence would put it on his own finger when no one was around. Then his father left, but the ring stayed, and he tried it on more often. His hands grew bigger. The ring wasn't quite so loose. It didn't feel so heavy.

Then, one day when he was fifteen, the ring, like his father, was gone.

"Got rid of it," his mother said. "Ugly old thing. And with that broken heart." She shook her head. "Bad luck, if you ask me."

"Where'd it go?" Spence had demanded, furious, desperate.

"Took all your father's stuff to the junk shop on Galena," his mother said. "Good riddance."

Spence hadn't cared about anything else, only the ring.

The lady in the junk shop had sold it back to him. "It's not really worth much," she'd said doubtfully when he'd insisted on buying it.

"It is to me," Spence said. It was the only thing he had that connected to a good family memory. The only thing that connected to his grandfather.

And he had given it to Sadie the night she'd married him?

What had he been thinking?

He didn't have time to figure it out, though, because at that moment the plane jolted down onto the runway.

And as it slowed, turned and taxied toward the terminal, Sadie took a deep breath. "All set?"

Spence nodded. He hoped to God he was. He still felt shaken.

Then everyone was getting up and moving out.

"Here," Sadie said as they edged toward the door. And he felt her press something into his palm. "You'll need this."

"Need what?" But he could feel the answer even as he asked.

A wedding ring.

His fingers instinctively closed around it. The edge of it dug into his palm. The rings he'd got for Sadie had been a token of appreciation. He never expected to receive one in return.

"It's called rose gold. It has copper in it," Sadie said when he stopped in the air bridge to stare at it, blocking the way for the other passengers trying to move around them. "It's not a big deal," she added. "But I thought maybe you'd want to—considering Leonie and all."

He hadn't been going to with Dena. But now he nodded. "Good idea."

Leonie would see it and know he was taken. Isogawa would see it and understand that he and Sadie were a pair. It made perfect sense.

He slid it on his finger.

He suddenly felt married.

And not a moment too soon, he thought, once they'd cleared customs and were headed to the charter-plane departure lounge.

Everyone else was already there. He knew both New Zealand couples, Steve Walker and his wife, Cathy, and John and Marion Ten Eyk were getting there the night before. And Richard and Leonie were there, too. The four kiwis were talking among themselves. Richard was, as usual, deeply engrossed in something on his laptop. But as soon as Leonie glanced up from a magazine and saw them coming, she squealed with delight.

"Spence! Darling!" She leaped out of her seat and rushed toward him, arms open wide.

He braced himself for the onslaught, ready to catch her and hold her at arm's length when other fingers suddenly slid into his hand, and Sadie was right there next to him saying smoothly, "Aren't you going to introduce us, dear?"

Dear? Spence opened his mouth and nothing came out.

It didn't matter. Sadie went right on. "Oh, I recognize your voice." She beamed at Leonie, who, apparently seeing Sadie's hand in his, had stopped inches from launching herself into Spence's arms. "You must be Leonie! I'm Sadie."

And she intercepted the hug meant for him and gave Leonie an enthusiastic one of her own.

"S-Sadie?" Leonie sputtered, stepping out of the embrace to look Sadie up and down. "You're *Sadie?* Spence's—"

"Wife," Spence said smoothly. He had his bearings now. "Sadie is my wife," he told Leonie, sliding his arm around Sadie's waist as he did so. "And you can be the first to congratulate us."

Shock, confusion, consternation and a whole host of other expressions skittered across Leonie's face.

"But Sadie…works for you." Leonie's wide blue eyes fastened on Sadie who withstood the scrutiny and didn't give an inch.

"She does. She did."

"It's like out of a romance novel," Sadie told the other woman cheerfully. "You know the ones—years go by and finally the boss wakes up and sees the woman underfoot all day for the woman she really is."

Leonie's eyes went wider still, then just a little doubtful. But at Sadie's determined pleasantness she could hardly do more than smile wistfully.

"Wow. Congratulations." Then she turned a half-sceptical, half-accusing gaze on him. "And you never said a word. Not a single clue. Richard!" She turned to call to her husband, "Guess what Spence has brought with him!"

"Contracts, I hope," Richard said vaguely, not glancing up.

"I'm sure he has, darling," Leonie said impatiently. "But he's also brought a wife!"

Richard's head came up then. "A wife? Tyack's got a wife?" He set the computer aside then and came straight over, his eyes studying Sadie all the way. From the appreciation on his face, Spence thought with annoyance, he apparently liked what he saw.

Richard offered Sadie a hand, kissed her on both cheeks, then beamed at her. "Married the boss, did you? Smart girl. Beautiful, too." He turned to Spence. "Got eyes in your head," he said approvingly. "And you're not stupid, either. This girl's the one who keeps the wheels turning at the home office, isn't she?"

"She does a good job," Spence said stiffly, wondering why Richard was still holding on to Sadie's hand. He scowled.

Sadie smiled and deftly extracted her hand and laid it on Spence's arm. "I try to keep him thinking that," she told the other man.

Richard laughed. "I'm sure you manage." He rubbed his hands together. "Glad we've got a week on the island. Great idea of Isogawa's. It'll give us lots of time to get to know each other better."

Spence stared. Was Carstairs hitting on Sadie?

"I'm sure we'll have plenty of opportunity to visit," Sadie replied easily. Her smile included Leonie, too. "I'm looking forward to it. And to meeting everyone else in person as well," she added as the Ten Eyks and Walkers came over.

Spence made the introductions, but Sadie already seemed to know them all.

"Of course I do," she said. "I made all the reservations. Marion and Cathy and I have spoken on the phone. Cathy's a weaver and Marion paints. She's done some murals like Martha, and next time Theo and Martha go to New Zealand they're going to visit Marion and John."

"They are?" Spence just stood there, somewhere between bemused and stunned, while his wife chatted with everyone as if she'd known them for ages—which apparently she had.

CHAPTER SIX

MR. ISOGAWA was at the dock to meet the seaplane when it landed.

A dapper man in his late sixties with steel-gray hair and a small bristly mustache, he was exactly as Spence had pictured him—a strict, soft-spoken field marshal—a man with Standards and Expectations.

He bowed and shook hands with Spence, but before Spence could introduce everyone, he said, "Come. We will go to the lodge. I will introduce you to my wife. She looks forward to meeting you. It is good you are all here. Nanumi is a place for families."

He made another bow, then he directed a small army of silent, smiling staff members to carry their luggage to various lodgings, then turned and led the way up a plank walkway toward a thatched roof Spence could see in the distance.

He turned and caught Sadie's eye. See?

Sadie smiled slightly and gave an infinitesimal nod in return.

The lodge when they came up on it, was a low-slung, sprawling, native wood, glass and thatch building that over-looked a crescent shaped bay. Spence had seen pictures of it, of course. But in person it was even more impressive than the pictures—not just a beautiful structure, but a harmonious ex-tension of the picture-postcard, Pacific-island paradise in which it was set. Beside him, Sadie seemed to draw in an awed breath.

Dena would barely have noticed it. She'd spent so much time in the Caribbean—her father owned an island there—that tropical beauty held no novelty for her.

But Sadie was clearly dazzled by the island, the resort and the lodge they were entering. It was a spacious high-ceilinged room, one side all glass and open air, facing the bay. A bamboo bar curved around one end, and groupings of chairs and sofas all upholstered in brightly colored Polynesian designs were arranged around low tables.

"Here we will sit," Mr. Isogawa gestured toward them. "And now you will introduce us, Spencer-san?"

Spence did. Mr. Isogawa smiled and bowed and, for good measure apparently, shook hands with each of the men and their wives. It was very cordial, very proper. And then Spence took Sadie by the hand and drew her forward.

"I would like you to meet my wife, Mr. Isogawa. This is Sadie."

"*Sadie?*" Mr. Isogawa's distant politeness vanished. He stared first at Spence, and then abruptly turned his gaze on Sadie. "This is Sadie? You are marrying *my* Sadie?"

"*Your* Sadie?" It was Spence's turn to stare as Mr. Isogawa reached out and tapped Sadie on the arm so that she turned to face him squarely.

Sadie was smiling broadly but almost shyly as she nodded. "Yes, he is. Married to me, I mean."

At which Mr. Isogawa clapped his hands together delightedly, then broke into a wide welcoming grin. He bowed now to Sadie—a much deeper bow than anyone else had merited—and then he grasped both Sadie's hands in his and began talking rapidly to her.

In Japanese.

Spence stared. "She doesn't—"

But apparently she did, because Sadie began talking, too. In Japanese.

"Since when," he demanded, "do you speak Japanese?"

Sadie finished whatever she was saying to Mr. Isogawa before she turned to him and shrugged lightly. "Remember Tammy Nakamura, my roommate at UCLA?"

"No." The most he remembered about Sadie at UCLA was how damned inconvenient it had been the four years she was there. Coming home in the summers had never been enough. What he remembered about UCLA was going down for her graduation and hauling her back to Butte!

"Tammy was Japanese-American. But her dad made sure all the kids could speak the language. I made her teach me. When you started doing business with Mr. Isogawa, I tried it out on him." She grinned. "He thinks I'm very clever."

Mr. Isogawa's head bobbed in agreement. "Sadie is very smart. Works very hard. Beautiful, too," he murmured. And he still, Spence noted, hadn't let go of Sadie's hands.

What was it with men and Sadie's hands?

Just then Mr. Isogawa said something else to her in Japanese, and she blushed and held out her left hand for his inspection.

Spence felt a prickling between his shoulder blades as Mr. Isogawa even lifted her finger to scrutinized them in silence. They were only simple jade rings. Folk art. Nothing valuable or even particularly beautiful. And it was obvious that Mr. Isogawa thought Sadie was both.

Spence suddenly wished he'd kept the rock from Tiffany's and had insisted that she wear it. Dena had known what she was doing. He, on the other hand, had let his business sense be blinded by knowing Sadie.

But then Mr. Isogawa smiled. And this was different than his earlier smiles. This one reached his eyes. It seemed to come from the inside out. He held Sadie's hand out for Spence to take.

Slowly Spence took it.

Then Mr. Isogawa looked at Sadie. *"Sono yubiwa, o'suki desuka?"*

"Do I like them?" she translated. "Oh yes!" She nodded vehemently. "I mean, *hai*. I certainly do."

The smile on his lined face deepened as Mr. Isogawa nodded. "I, too." He turned his gaze on Spence, his gaze searching. "I see you chose well."

And Spence didn't think he was talking about the rings at all. His face felt suddenly hot. "I think so. I'm glad you agree."

Still smiling, Mr. Isogawa nodded. Then he turned and beckoned to a woman hovering in shadows on the far side of the lounge. She was about the same age as he was, very petite and beautifully dressed in a silk sarong that seemed to reflect all the colors of the sea.

"My wife," Mr. Isogawa said, "Toshiko."

One by one he introduced her to all of them. And when he got to Sadie, the woman's eyes lit up and Sadie's did, too. They bowed and smiled very properly, and then they were holding hands and talking like old friends.

"I suppose you've met Mrs. Isogawa, too," he muttered.

Sadie laughed. "Sort of. We met on the phone. She's learning English. When Mr. Isogawa told me, I offered to help. We practice together, don't we?" she said slowly in English so the other woman could understand.

"Sadie is a good teacher." Mrs. Isogawa's voice was soft but her pronunciation was clear and precise. "Very smart."

"So I see." Spence was seeing more than he'd ever imagined.

While he'd been putting this deal together, he'd been all over the world, keeping tabs on other deals, as well. He'd sent Sadie the specs and the background and what he hoped to accomplish, and then he'd said she should keep track of things and get in touch with the various people he'd contacted. Then he'd left her to it.

He'd never considered how much contact she'd had, how much work she'd done. He'd just assumed everything had fallen into place because of his intuition and groundwork. Now he saw that Mr. Isogawa's willingness to consider a bunch of western investors was more because Sadie had provided such diligent hands-on care and friendship than because he was a brilliant strategist and had put together a good group.

"We'll practice while I'm here," Sadie was saying now, and Mrs. Isogawa nodded happily.

But then Mr. Isogawa began speaking rapidly to his wife in their own language. Her eyes widened and she looked from Sadie to Spence and then to the rings on Sadie's hand as if seeing them for the first time.

"You are married?"

"Yes, we're married," Sadie agreed.

"Newlyweds," Leonie drawled. "So sweet."

"On their honeymoon," Mr. Isogawa decided happily.

"Well, not really." Sadie shook her head and wrapped her arms across her chest.

But Mr. Isogawa had other ideas. He called to the barman for champagne, then spoke to another man who nodded and disappeared quickly out the door. In a matter of seconds bottles of bubbly appeared, were opened and poured, and everyone was handed a flute.

"And now we will toast your happiness," Mr. Isogawa said. He raised his glass and spoke first in Japanese, then in English. Spence had no idea what he'd said in Japanese, but in English he wished them a long life, great wealth, deep happiness and many children.

"Many many children," he heard Mrs. Isogawa echo, then she smiled at Sadie and giggled.

Sadie blushed.

"Many many many children," Leonie agreed sotto voce. "Wouldn't you love lots of little kiddies, Spence?"

Sadie looked like she wanted to disappear through the floor.

"You're embarrassing the girl," Richard said brusquely. "Let them decide how many they're gonna have in private. But I'll drink to the rest of it. To Spence and Sadie. Congratulations and best wishes."

Fortunately, once the toast had been drunk, attention shifted. Sadie asked about the building, and Mr. Isogawa began to talk about the concept, the furnishings, the native artists whose work was displayed on a rotating basis, the local woods and textiles that were used as much as possible in the upholstery and bedding.

"We try," he said, "to give our guests the very best of this world. We do not let the outside intrude. We make a haven of beauty, as you say?" He looked to Sadie for affirmation that he had the right words.

"Indeed you have," Sadie agreed, running her hand lightly over the back of one of the sofas.

"And your quarters even more, I think. You will see." He glanced up as the young man who had disappeared through the doorway now reappeared. "And as soon as you are ready, Jale will show you to your *bures*." He turned to Spence. "We did not know you were bringing a new wife. This is special."

"Anything is fine," Spence assured him. "Sadie and I don't care."

"I care. Toshiko and I had moved into the honeymoon *bure* because it is small. Intimate. Only for two. Not for families. We did not realize we would have real honeymooners with us. So we'll make a change."

"We don't—" Spence began.

"It's not necessary—" Sadie said quickly.

But Mr. Isogawa raised a hand to silence them both. "It is necessary. *Shinkon-san ni, tekishite imasu.*"

Spence blinked, then looked at Sadie to see if she understood.

"He says it's appropriate," Sadie translated quietly. "He wants us to stay there because it's the appropriate place for newlyweds."

"But we're not on our honeymoon," Spence protested. "We're here on business. We're here to come to terms on the resort."

"But why is the resort at all?" Mr. Isogawa asked simply.

Spence shook his head, confused. "What?"

"We make the resort for couples. For families. To come together," Mr. Isogawa explained. "To remember, yes? Nanumi. To remind ourselves of what is most important. Business, yes, of course we do business. But business is only a part of life," Mr. Isogawa said. "The less important part. You understand?" His dark eyes seemed to bore into the depths of Spence's soul.

"I— Yes."

He understood the concept, at least.

His family had had no idea. The ring he'd given Sadie had been his only experience of that sort of connection. It had been a sign of his great-grandfather's love. A love which had endured loneliness and then death. But his own father had ignored it, had left it sitting in a saucer on the bureau. His mother had, typically, thrown it out.

But Mr. Isogawa was smiling at Sadie—and Sadie was smiling, too, just like she was thrilled, like she was his real wife.

"All right," Spence said. "But we are here for business."

Mr. Isogawa bowed. "Later we will talk business. Now you must share the beginning of your marriage with your beautiful wife."

The honeymoon *bure* was like *Swiss Family Robinson* meets *Modern Bride*.

Sadie stood in the open doorway and looked around in amazement. All of the resort's *bures* or native bungalows had looked beautiful as they'd passed them. But this one, inside and out, was spectacular.

It was a *bure* and not quite a *bure*. A thatched island cottage, yes, but it was built in a tree—like a treehouse. Not cobbled on, either, but exquisitely interwoven so that the *bure* seemed to flow between the branches. The room seemed carved out of the tree, not perched in it.

"Not traditional," Mr. Isogawa had apologized. "But we think, nice."

Nice didn't being to cover it.

The *bure* was nestled a dozen steps up in the spread of a vast tree that Sadie couldn't identify. From the frond-covered front porch with its gently swinging hammock to the interior native hardwood floors and *kiao* mats, from the vast king-size bed— "Almost as big as Kansas," she murmured—to the private open-air waterfall shower and spa hidden from the beach by carefully placed bamboo screens, it was elegant and spacious. With its stunningly printed tapa cloth wall hangings and the airy wicker table and chairs under the window and a pair of sturdy uphol-stered kauri chairs, it was exotic yet homey and welcoming at the same time. With views of a sand-and-sea paradise out of every door and window, it was beyond anything she had ever imagined.

"I hope you will be very happy here." The young man who had brought them along the wooden pathway that threaded through the trees now bowed slightly and left them alone. Together.

In the honeymoon *bure*—with one room. And one bed.

"Well, isn't this nice?" she said brightly when Spence didn't say anything at all.

He hadn't said a word since they'd left the main lodge. He'd followed the man called Jale—which Sadie had figured out was the local version of Charlie—down the path in silence. Ordinarily Spence peppered people with questions. He rarely had a thought he didn't share. But he'd taken in all the *bure's* amenities in complete silence. And even after Jale left he didn't speak.

Now he said abruptly, "We'll have to share the bed. I can't

sleep in the hammock." He jerked his head toward the one swinging lightly on the porch outside the door.

"I know."

"Isogawa would notice. Or the help would. They'd comment. We can't take the chance."

"I know."

He didn't seem to hear. He cracked his knuckles and began to pace. "All the other *bures* have two beds!"

"Don't worry about it," Sadie said. "I'll stay on my own side. I promise I won't molest you."

He stopped dead. "What?"

"I said, I promise not to attack you!"

It was Spence's turn to blink. "That's not what I meant," he said gruffly. "I promised you two beds."

You promised to love, honor and cherish me for the rest of our lives, too, Sadie thought. But she didn't say it.

"I was there the whole time. I could almost see what was going through Mr. Isogawa's head. He was determined to make this special for us."

"You don't mind?"

"I'll live," Sadie assured him. "Will you?"

"Of course! It will be fine."

But even as he spoke, he moved away from the bed, as if determined to put as much space as he could between it and himself for as long as possible.

Sadie tried not to notice. With her thumb she turned the rings on her fingers. The rings proved that on some level at least Spence understood her, cared about her. And the *bure*—well, she was going to take it as a sign that someone, besides the Isogawas, wanted her and Spence to be together.

She kicked off her sandals and flexed her toes against the cool wooden floor. "How about a swim?" she suggested.

Spence glanced at the bed. "A swim sounds fine," he said

quickly. "You go ahead and change. And I'll— Oh, hell, I left my briefcase up at the lodge. I'll go up and get it."

"You'd better be sure not to stay up there and work."

"No." He went out, then stopped on the porch and turned back. "Sade? Thanks."

She cocked her head. "Thanks?"

"I knew everything on this deal was coming together smoothly. I never realized how much of it was thanks to you. Your connections with all of them—the Isogawas, the Walkers, the Ten Eyks, even Richard and Leonie—are what has made this work so far."

"I've enjoyed it all," Sadie said truthfully. "It's been fun. They're interesting people."

"Yeah. They are. But I want you to know I appreciate it." He hesitated, as if he might say something else. Then he just muttered, "Thanks," again, and turned and hurried up the path.

She watched until he disappeared among the palms and then she sank down on the bed and sighed. He'd noticed her relationships with the Isogawas, the Ten Eyks, the Walkers. He *appreciated* them. He *thanked* her for them!

He probably even thought she'd developed them for the good of the company and for no other reason at all.

Sometimes Spencer Tyack was too stupid to live. And before the week was over, she just might kill him.

But—Sadie smiled—since he'd brought her to paradise, she might as well take a swim first.

Sadie swam.

John and Marion joined her. They found the water warm and inviting. Waves were almost nonexistent. It was like a gorgeous peaceful turquoise bath, breathtakingly clear and beautiful.

Spence never came.

"Working," Marion guessed.

"Damn fool," John said.

Was he? Sadie wondered. Or was he just avoiding her? She swam or lazed on the sand for over an hour. He never appeared.

"Richard probably got him," John said. "Trapped him somewhere. Doing ten-year projections. He's even a bigger workaholic than Spence."

Richard? Or had Leonie waylaid him on his way to the lodge?

All of a sudden Sadie thought she'd better go check. "I'll just go have a look," she said.

"You do that. Grab him by the ear and bring him down," Marion suggested.

"Or find something better to do." John grinned and gave her a conspiratorial wink.

Sadie blushed. "Yes, um…maybe I'll do that."

She waggled her fingers in farewell, wrapped the towel around her middle and made her way up the pathway to the treehouse. She could see the door was open when she reached the steps. So no Richard and, presumably, no Leonie.

He was either working or avoiding her.

"Spence? If Mr. Isogawa finds out that you're up here working—" She stopped dead.

He wasn't working. He was fast asleep.

Apparently he had actually intended to come down to the beach because a pair of black swimming trunks lay on the bed beside him. His feet were bare, his shirt unbuttoned. His lips parted slightly. And through them Sadie heart the faintest of snores.

"Spence?" she said, quietly this time, more to be sure that he really was sound asleep than to try to wake him.

He didn't respond. Not even an eyelash flickered.

She shouldn't be surprised, Sadie realized. While she had slept on the flight, he had apparently worked the whole time. And before that flight, she remembered, he'd already flown into

L.A. from New York, a longer journey than hers, over more time zones. No wonder he was exhausted.

And damnably hard to resist, Sadie thought, as she stood looking down at him, drinking in the sight.

He might have been a different man from the one she knew awake. The fierce intensity that so characterized his every waking moment was gone. His mouth was softer. The rest of his face, too, seemed more relaxed. Gentler.

His five-o'clock shadow had gone another twelve hours and was rougher and darker than ever. Sadie remembered the brush of his whiskered jaw against hers when they'd made love the night they'd married. She hadn't touched that stubble since. She felt a compulsion to reach down and brush her hand against his cheek now.

She didn't. Couldn't let herself. This week was roller-coaster ride enough. She didn't need to make it worse. So she tucked her arms across her chest and trapped her hands in case they got the best of her.

Just look, don't touch.

But this Spence was so much more clearly the person she knew was inside the one the world saw that she almost couldn't help herself. In him now she saw hints of the boy she remembered—and of the man she'd married that night four years ago.

When they'd got back to the room, they had made love eagerly, desperately, frantically, barely making it to the bed as they'd torn each other's clothes off as they went. Their lovemaking had been scorching.

And afterward he had murmured, "It should always have been you." And then, almost instantly, he had fallen asleep in her arms.

And Sadie had watched him sleep.

She had lain awake, astonished at the sudden turn in direction her life had taken, afraid to close her eyes lest when she awoke it would all turn out to be a dream.

And when she finally did go to sleep, she'd awakened a few hours later to find that it had become a nightmare.

Still, she remembered this part as vividly as if it had happened only hours before. Remembered how she'd held him close, relishing the brush of his soft hair against her nose, loving the feel of the rough whiskers on his jaw against the smoothness of her cheek.

She'd feathered kisses there. And Spence had sighed and smiled, had moved his mouth as if to kiss her back, but in the end had slept on.

She saw that man asleep here now, and she could only remember the night—not the morning after. It was all she could do to hug her arms against her chest to stop them reaching out for him.

Go on, Martha whispered inside her head. *What are you waiting for?*

But as much as she would have loved to lie down beside him and wrap her arms around him, Sadie couldn't do it.

He had to want it; he had to want her; and she had to know it.

She started to move away, but couldn't quite do it. Not without, for just a moment, freeing a hand to reach down and let it drift lightly over his ruffled dark hair.

"I love you," she whispered.

It was only the truth—as much as it hurt to think her love might never be returned.

Spence smiled. And he slept.

There was a regular tub in the bathroom that would afford her privacy. But just beyond the sliding glass doors there was a small, screened outdoor patio with a rainforestlike shower that fell into a rock pool.

Sadie had been able to resist sharing the bed with Spence— at least for the moment—but a rainforest shower was too much temptation. He would never know. He was dead to the world. So she fetched a towel from the bathroom and one of the thick terry-cloth robes there, too. Carrying the rose-colored robe and the towel, she padded back quietly through the bedroom to slide open the doors.

Spence had rolled onto his side. But his breathing was still deep and even.

Sadie watched him, assessed the room on the bed and decided that, if he stayed where he was, there would be room for her to slide into the bed when she'd showered. That shouldn't offend his sensibilities too much.

She stepped out onto the decking and eased the door shut behind her. With a quick self-conscious glance back at the sleeping Spence, she wriggled out of her swimsuit. Feeling even more self-conscious and enormously decadent, she stepped into the pool and beneath the shower.

It was heaven. The spray was soft and full, the water lukewarm—absolutely perfect. She tipped her head back and let the spray hit her face, slide down her neck and over the rest of her body.

"Ah, yes." She smiled, turned, let it course down her back. Reaching for one of the tubes lined up along the rock shelf, she squeezed out a dollop of the pineapple-scented shampoo and worked it into her hair, then rinsed it and watched as blobs of lather slid down her arms and over her breasts and plopped into the pool which seemed to be filling with bubbles.

Decadent didn't even begin to describe it. She would never take a shower again in her utilitarian claw-foot tub back in Butte without remembering this one.

Once more she lifted her face into the spray and let it wash over her whole body. A gentle sea breeze stirred the air and the surrounding tree leaves. In the distance she could hear people's voices on the beach. Marion and John seemed to have been joined by Steve and Cathy and Leonie. They were laughing about something. It felt odd to be able to hear them so clearly, be so close—and so naked—and know they couldn't see her.

Or could they?

Sadie craned her neck to look over the top of the screen to make sure. But they weren't looking her way at all. She was completely hidden.

No one saw her.

Except Spence.

CHAPTER SEVEN

SPENCE was dreaming.

They were vibrant vivid dreams in which he was undressing Sadie, then kissing his way up her arms and across her shoulders, along her jawline, all over her cheeks, the tip of her nose and, finally, her luscious beautiful mouth.

And all the while he was kissing her, he was running his hands over her and dispensing with her clothes, her proper tailored blouses and jackets, eager to get to the peach-colored scraps of silk he knew were underneath.

Then, just when he reached the silk and began to unhook her bra, he heard the faint click of the hook.

Click? Of the hook?

He jerked. His eyes opened as Sadie clicked open the sliding glass door to the enclosed shower room. Then the door clicked shut again. And through it Spence beheld a reality more vibrant and vivid than all his dreams and fantasies of Sadie in peach-colored underwear.

As he watched in dazed but dazzled fascination, the real-live Sadie Morrissey hung her towel and robe on a hook by the waterfall, then with a quick glance toward the door, turned and peeled down her swimsuit and stepped naked into the water.

His mouth went dry. His eyes didn't blink as he stared at a peach-colored Sadie wearing nothing at all!

He groaned at the sight, at the instant reaction of his body, already primed by his dreams. Sucking in a harsh breath, Spence shut his eyes.

"Damn." He swallowed, then opened his eyes a fraction, hoping against hope that he'd imagined it all, that jet lag and stress and overwork and sexual frustration—not to mention Sadie frustration—had combined to create hallucinations.

Not so.

She was still there. Standing in the shallow rock pool beneath the spray, then doing a little hop-skip, a little dance step, like some water sprite. Her breasts bounced lightly, the water made her skin glisten. He swallowed again.

He couldn't close his eyes now. There was no point. Why bother? He was never going to be able to forget this. He might as well enjoy the show.

She was, after all, his wife.

So he was entitled, right?

He could get up off this bed and strip off his clothes and join her there in the pool under the shower. As her husband, he could run his hands over her soap-slicked body. He could kiss her neck, could kiss his way down across her breasts, could touch his tongue to her navel, kiss lower, touch her—there.

His jaw clenched and he rolled onto his back, his body screaming a protest at not being allowed to do exactly that, at not being allowed to do more.

Why *not* do more?

Was she going to fight him off? She hadn't been as upset about there being only one bed as he had. And he'd been upset because he thought it mattered to her.

Didn't it?

Did she *want* him to make love to her?

She'd married him, hadn't she? his body argued.

But she'd only married him under duress, his brain replied. Because he'd made it impossible for her to refuse. Because she'd cared about him as a friend, because he'd been at the end of his rope and, knowing it, she'd done him a favor. Because she'd *pitied* him!

And why would she want to be married to him, anyway? She knew his family. She knew his background. She knew as well as Danny ever had what poor husband material he was. She was a forever woman—a woman who had always wanted a husband, a home and a family.

She deserved a far better man than him.

So the least he could do was keep his mind on business. He just needed to remember that.

But right now he needed to get out of here.

Spence knew human nature—especially his own—well enough to know that all the rational resolutions in the world could fail in the face of too much temptation.

His father hadn't taught him much. But he'd damn sure taught him that.

He wasn't there!

Sadie had finished her shower, dried off and wrapped herself in the soft rose-colored terry robe. She'd combed her fingers through her hair so she didn't look like a complete scarecrow, and then, taking a deep breath, carefully and quietly as possible, she'd slid open the glass door, hoping Spence had left her a corner of the bed in which to nap.

And he wasn't there! The bed was empty, the coverlet rumpled, but Spence was gone.

Heart slamming against her chest, Sadie ran to the bathroom. He wasn't there. She peered out onto the front deck. No Spence.

She even went out and looked down toward the beach. But everyone had gone. It was empty now, too.

She couldn't see or hear a single soul, only the sound of the sea as it washed against the shore and the rustle of the breeze in the palms.

Where had he gone?

And why?

His swim trunks were missing. The clothes he'd been wearing were hanging in the closet. Had he awakened and grabbed his trunks, thinking she was still down at the beach?

Had he not seen her in the shower?

Naked in the shower!

How could he not? Her face burned as she realized there was simply no way he could not have seen her. While the view from the waterfall into the room was obscured by the sun's reflection on the glass, the view of the shower area was crystal clear.

He couldn't have missed her.

Her whole body was hot now. Burning from humiliation, not the possibility of embarrassment.

He had seen her and looked the other way. *Run* the other way!

She wanted to die. How could she spend a week with Spence in the same room—in the same bed—if he couldn't even bear to look at her?

And she'd hoped to make a real marriage out of this?

What had she been thinking? The very thought seemed laughable now.

And the joke, Sadie knew, was on her.

The sound of drumbeats, deep and hollow, echoed off the wall of the *bure* late that afternoon. Sadie knew what they meant—that the lounge and bar were open, that dinner would soon be served.

And of course she had to be there. It was her job.

For the past two hours she had sat huddled in one of the

wicker chairs in the *bure* crying. It was stupid. Pointless. She told herself that over and over. But it didn't help.

She hadn't any idea where Spence was. Wherever he had gone to, desperate to get away from her nakedness, he had never returned.

He would have to show up at dinner, though. It was a command performance, one of the places Mr. Isogawa was sure to expect to see them together. So Spence would turn up, expecting her to act the part of the loving wife.

"How about the spurned wife?" she muttered, scrubbing at her eyes with a tissue. She wondered if this was how Leonie felt.

Probably. Damn men, anyway.

Still furious, Sadie wiped her eyes, then carefully applied a bit of makeup, hoping it would mask the worst of the blotchiness on her face. Her eyes were still red, but she could always say they were bloodshot from swimming. It wasn't a great excuse, but it was good enough.

Then she went to the closet and took out the red-orange wildly printed sundress Martha had brought over the morning Sadie had been leaving.

"It's seen Greece," Martha had said, thrusting it at her. "I wore it there when Theo and Eddy and I went back a few months ago. Theo thought it was *trés* sexy." She'd wiggled her eyebrows and grinned. "Maybe Spence will, too. Anyway, it should see the South Pacific before it retires."

And so it would, Sadie decided. She would do her job, and she would enjoy herself as best she could. The hell with Spence. But she owed it to Martha to give her dress a whirl.

She arrived by herself, and Mr. Isogawa, who with his wife had been visiting with the Ten Eyks, rose quickly and came over to bow and invite her to join them.

"You are enjoying yourself?" he asked.

"Yes, thank you. *Arigato*," she repeated in Japanese, making Mrs. Isogawa smile. "I'm having a wonderful time. The tree-house *bure* is magnificent. And I've been swimming already. The beach is beautiful, the water was so warm. And the water-fall in the spa—I loved it."

She must have been convincing because he smiled. "And Spencer? Did Spencer enjoy? Where is Spencer?"

"Spencer fell asleep," she reported with absolute honesty. "He was so tired after working on the plane all the way down here, he just collapsed. I went swimming without him. And when he woke up, I guess he went out exploring on his own."

And when he showed up, he could damned well tell Mr. Isogawa all about it. What she'd said was the truth—minus her own interpretation of it.

Mr. Isogawa nodded. "I will be interested to hear what he found."

What Spence found, they learned, when he arrived just before dinner was served, was that there was a track up the hill through the bush to a lookout area at the top from which you could see virtually the whole island.

"It has amazing 360-degree views. Blows your mind." He looked bright-eyed and handsome as sin, well rested and com-pletely at ease.

Sadie hated him.

He must have gone back to the treehouse after she'd left, because he had changed clothes and now wore a pair of tropic-weight khaki-colored trousers and a deep blue polo shirt that exactly matched the color of his eyes, though she was sure he had no idea.

"You had a good time, then?" She did her best to sound as cheerful and upbeat as he did, determined that she would do what she'd signed on for.

"Yep." He paused. "Sorry I didn't make it down swimming.

I conked out. I was going to join you, but you weren't swimming anymore when I woke up,"

No, I was naked in the shower. You could have joined me there. But of course she didn't say it. She just pasted a bright smile on her face and hoped she looked sincere.

"I'll take you there tomorrow," he said "You'll love it." And smiling down at her, he slung an arm around her shoulders and drew her hard against him.

The self-preserving part of Sadie wanted to stiffen and resist. The furious part wanted to kick him where it would do the most good. He was such a convincing liar!

But she'd given her word, and to fight now would be disastrous not just for the deal, but it would make everyone uncomfortable. So she leaned into his embrace and smiled. "I'm sure I will."

Then, because she was damned if he was going to be the only one who showed how devoted they were, she turned her face toward his, and kissed him lightly on the jaw.

It was Spence who stiffened then, and she saw a flicker of confusion in his gaze, followed by something that looked like determined challenge. And the next thing she knew Spence bent his head and kissed her full on the lips!

It wasn't a passionate kiss, one that should have been saved for the privacy of a honeymoon *bure,* but it lingered long enough to be possessive, and it promised a host of things that left Sadie startled—and shaken—when at last Spence stepped away.

He smiled at her.

She shot him a furious glare, then looked up to see Leonie Carstairs watching.

The meaning of the kiss was suddenly perfectly clear. It was a "keep your distance" kiss, meant for Leonie. He'd intended it to mean nothing to Sadie. Nothing at all.

"Come," Mr. Isogawa said. "It is time for dinner." He took his wife's arm and led her toward the dining room.

Spence, still smiling, held out his arm to her.

And Sadie, after one careful steadying breath, slipped her arm through his and, ignoring her heartache, walked by his side to the dinner table.

"Well, that went well," Spence said briskly as he opened the door to their *bure* after an excellent dinner and an evening of general "getting to know you better" conversation.

"Do you think so?" Sadie said ironically, because, while she'd done her best, she didn't think *well* described it. *Hypocritcal* came closer.

Now she brushed past him into the room, then immediately wished she hadn't.

The bed, which had seemed Kansas-size a few short hours ago, now appeared only slightly larger than a postage stamp. And it was one thing to go to bed with a man you loved if you thought he might find you appealing, and another to go to bed with a man who had turned and run when he'd glimpsed you naked.

And now there was no beach to escape to, no grounds to wander about it. It was all darkness—velvety black with amazing stars and constellations she had enjoyed learning about from John Ten Eyk. But she couldn't stay out there all night.

"Didn't you think so?" Spence sounded surprised. He shut the door and kicked off his shoes. "Everybody was having a good time. The place is in terrific shape, a lot better than I expected. The service seems very good. The food was fantastic."

"Yes."

"Leonie left me alone," Spence said with supreme satisfaction. "And when you get past the starchiness, Isogawa's a nice guy. So's his wife. And they obviously think you're wonderful. So do I," he said cheerfully.

"Why? Because I scared off Leonie? Because your clever plan is working? Isn't that just great."

Spence's forehead furrowed as his brows drew down. "What's the matter with you?"

"Nothing's the matter with me! Nothing at all."

"I can tell. You're so full of sweetness and light tonight." Spence rolled his eyes.

"You don't know anything about me!"

"So, tell me. Why are you mad?"

His simple question infuriated her even more. "Who said I was mad?" Sadie spun away, putting the bed between them, as he came toward her.

"Lucky guess," he drawled. Their gazes met across the bed, his stony and furious, hers equally mad. He raked a hand through his hair and scowled deeply. "So, let me venture a guess."

She lifted a shoulder indifferently. "Suit yourself."

"It's about this afternoon. Isn't it?" he prodded, when she didn't reply at once.

"What do you think?"

"I think I'm doing the best I can, damn it," he snapped. "All right, fine, I apologize! But I'm not blind, Sadie! If you don't pull the drapes across the windows, I'm going to get an eyeful. I can't help it! But I left, didn't I?"

Sadie's jaw dropped. *"What?"*

Still Spence glowered, eyes flashing. "If you didn't want me to see you naked, why the hell did you leave the drapes open when you took your shower?"

That was what he thought she was mad about? That he had seen her naked? Not that he had been so disgusted by the sight that he'd left the room?

"Well?" he demanded when she didn't reply.

Numbly Sadie shook her head, still trying to fathom that, make sense of it. Finally she could only ask dumbly, "That's why you left?"

"Did you want me to lie there staring at you? Is our Sadie an exhibitionist now?" His tone was mocking.

"Of course not! I needed a shower. I'd come in from swimming in the ocean. It was beautiful, inviting. Not like the bathtub I can use every day. And *you* were *asleep!* I wasn't trying to seduce you!"

"Which is exactly what I figured," he informed her flatly. "And I didn't imagine you would be any less enticing when you came back in the room." Hard blue eyes met hers. "So I left."

But Sadie was stuck a sentence earlier. "Enticing?" She echoed the word as if she had never heard it before. Was he saying. "You thought I was…?" She stared at him in wonderment.

"You're enticing as hell, Sadie Morrissey," he bit out. "And while I would have loved to lie there watching you cavorting under the shower—"

"I was *not* cavorting!" she protested.

"No? Well, dancing then. Hopping around. You hopped." He made it sound like an accusation.

God, how long had he watched? Sadie felt herself go scarlet.

"You enticed," he said again, very firmly. "And I wouldn't have been content with looking. I would have wanted more. And that wasn't part of our bargain. So I left."

Oh.

"So I apologize," he said tersely. "It was all I could think to do at the time."

"All?" Sadie said before she could stop herself.

Their gazes met again, locked this time. Electricity arced between them. Desire. Hunger. Frustration. Need. Sadie certainly felt all of them. She had no idea what Spence felt at his end.

He gritted his teeth. "Don't tempt me, Sadie. Little girls who play with matches are likely to get burned."

It was as if she'd been cut free, her fears banished, her heart hammering. "Is that a promise?"

"Cut it out," he said, his voice sharp. "Get ready for bed. I've already apologized for the bed, and I'm damned if I'll do it again."

"I don't care," Sadie said.

He ignored her. "I'll go out and walk on the beach while you're changing. Flick the light when you're decent and all tucked in." Then, without letting her reply, he opened the door and stalked out into the night.

He stood outside looking up into the night sky, telling himself it would be all right.

He'd survived the evening. He'd played his part well and so had Sadie. Yes, there had been a few tense moments, but he'd handled things well. He'd apologized for this afternoon—not that it had been his fault, damn it—and he'd got out before Sadie could misinterpret anything else.

If he was lucky, she'd just go to bed and fall asleep at once. She hadn't had any rest as far as he knew. Maybe she'd slept this afternoon after her shower, but the bed looked pretty much the way it had when he'd decamped. So she ought, by rights, to be exhausted.

Spence prayed that she'd be exhausted. He certainly was. By design. It was the only way he knew that he could get any sleep in a bed with Sadie Morrissey. He'd left the room this afternoon and he'd walked miles. Literally. He doubted there were many trails on the island that he hadn't explored.

So he could spend the night with her. Of course he could. It wasn't like he was a teenager anymore. He had control.

Then, out of the corner of his eye, he saw the light in their *bure* blink on and off—and all of a sudden his control didn't seem so certain.

Quit, he told himself sharply. *You never get anywhere by anticipating disaster. It will be fine. Give it five minutes. She'll be sound asleep.*

So he waited. He tried very hard not to think about peach-colored underwear and naked Sadie Morrisseys. He directed his mind firmly *away* from whatever Sadie might be wearing, tucked under the covers.

Mind over matter. He could do that. He climbed the steps and opened the door.

She wasn't under the covers at all!

"I told you to get in bed!"

Sadie smiled and stretched languorously. "I don't work for you 24/7. Sorry, but it's after hours."

He glared at her, furious at the enticement she provided sitting there on the bed in some flimsy little short yellow night-gown, all smiling and sweet, as tempting as Eve and her damned apple.

"What are you trying to do?" he demanded.

"To do?" She looked at him guilelessly.

He didn't believe the pose for a minute. "You're flaunting yourself! Trying to tempt me!" He flung words as accusations.

She smiled slightly. "Is it working?"

"What the hell do you think…? Damn it, Sadie! Do you want me to attack you?"

There was a half-second's hesitation. Then she gave him an impish smile. "As a matter of fact, I would."

CHAPTER EIGHT

"SADIE?" HE LOOKED as if he hadn't heard her right. As if he doubted his ears. She couldn't repeat it. So she said nervously, "Unless you'd rather not."

He stared at her. "You're kidding, aren't you?" His voice was ragged. And without another word, he dragged her into his arms, gathered her close, fastened his lips on hers.

He kissed her.

And instinctively Sadie kissed him back.

It was like coming home.

It was an echo of that earlier night—their wedding night—but infinitely better. Those kisses had been hungry and anxious and desperate. Frantic, almost. This kiss was hungry, too. Maybe even a little desperate.

But the similarity ended there. It didn't plunder; it explored. It didn't demand, it sought a response. And even more than that, it offered. It offered her Spence the way she had always dreamed of him. This kiss said he was hers.

Sadie, of course, had been his for as long as she could remember. But until now—until this moment—she'd been afraid that she had given herself wholly and completely to a man who, except for one brief night, would never want more from her than casual friendship and a lot of hard hours at work.

But in his kiss now, in the fine tremor of his hands as he touched her, she knew her fears were baseless. He wanted her every bit as much as she wanted him.

"Sadie." He whispered her name against her lips. She could taste it, taste the mingling of her name and him.

She smiled. "Mmm." She murmured, heady with pleasure as she tugged his shirt up and over his head, then let her hands roam over his arms, his shoulders, the hard muscular breadth of his back. "Yes."

"Yes? Like this?" he asked. His own hands were busy learning her. Touching her. Delighting her.

But he had much more access to her than she did to him. And she reached for the buckle of his belt, but fumbled it. "Lack of experience," she muttered as he undid it for her, then quickly shucked them and the rest of his clothes, and she could see him in all his naked glory.

"Oh yes," she whispered, pulling back to look, then reaching out to touch, to run her fingers lightly over his chest and across his hard abdomen, to brush lightly against his erection.

He tensed. "Sadie!" Her name hissed between his teeth.

"Mmm?" But he didn't answer as she pressed kisses against his jaw, his neck, his shoulders, his chest. His breathing grew faster, shallower. His skin was so hot she wondered if he had a fever. Against her hand she could feel the gallop of his heart. Still no answer, just a strangled sound from deep in his throat. Worriedly Sadie asked, "Are you…all right?"

The sound turned into something between a laugh and a moan. "I'm dying."

The ragged tone of his voice had her pulling back, horrified. "Dying?"

"For you, idiot," he muttered. "I've *been* dying for you."

Sadie didn't believe that for a minute. But she didn't mind him saying it. Actually she loved him saying it. "You're sure?"

He pressed her back onto the bed, his body coming full length against hers, settling in, fitting perfectly. "What do you think?"

"Oh." She understood now. She smiled, wriggled against him.

"Stop that." Spence's lips were against her mouth. "You're going to push me over the edge."

"What a shame," Sadie murmured, a delicious smile curving her mouth.

"Tease." Spence's lips moved from her lips over her cheeks. They touched, they pressed, they stroked, they nibbled. They teased and made her burn, too. There was a fine tremor in his fingers as they skimmed up her legs and caught hold of the nightgown, then tugged it up and over her head and tossed it away.

"Spence!"

He raised his head. "What? You wanted to wear it?"

"Yes. No. I don't care, Spence. I—"

He kissed her. "Shh. Lie back and think of Montana."

"No." She was absolutely not going to do that. She was going to participate. Completely. "I get to…to do things, too."

"Oh, really?" His mouth was so close she felt his breath on her cheek.

"Yes, really."

"I thought I was the boss."

"Only in the office. We're not in the office now."

"Now, wait a minute!"

But Sadie was done with waiting. She kissed him to shut him up, then drew her tongue along his lips and dipped it inside. At the same time she ran her hands down his back and over the solid curve of his buttocks, reveling as she did so in the fact that she finally felt free to touch him the way she'd wanted to touch him for years.

"Got a problem with this?" she asked him, wriggling again.

"I think I could get used to it," he muttered, then buried his face in her breasts only to lift his head a moment later and grin at her. And she could hear the awe in his voice when he said, "It really is you, Sadie. It really is you."

"It is." Though after all these years, she could hardly believe it, either.

Then Spence stopped talking once more. He kissed her thoroughly. His hands were everywhere, learning her lines and curves and secrets, making her gasp and squirm. And even though he had her gasping, she was determined to do the same for him.

Four years ago she'd been so overwhelmed by the sudden and bewildering turn of events and their astonishing marriage that she'd done little more than give herself to him. Now she wanted to do more, have more, share more.

And so she touched and stroked. She kissed and nuzzled. And Spence's control was snapped. His breathing quickened. His heart slammed.

"Sadie! Slow—!"

"No! I want you."

"I want...you...too. But I need—" He didn't finish, just pushed away to get off the bed.

"What?" Sadie stared after him, stunned.

But in a moment he'd found what he was looking for in his suitcase. Protection. They didn't need it, Sadie wanted to tell him. She'd be thrilled if she conceived here in this wonderful place.

But Spence had already accomplished the task and was settling between her legs again, finding the center of her, stroking, nudging, probing.

And Sadie took him in.

It had been so long. Sometimes she had despaired of ever having him again, of ever knowing this feeling of completion, of fulfillment. Sometimes, in fact, she thought she'd dreamed it.

But she hadn't. Oh, dear heaven, no, she hadn't! And she knew it now as she drew him into the heart of her being and wrapped him in the wonder of her love.

And then she knew nothing more—only the hot shuddering release of passion and tension and the sensation that at last the two of them had finally become one.

He owed her better than this. More than this. And Spence knew it.

He should have been slower, gentler, more thoughtful. He felt boneless, weightless, though he was sure he must be pressing Sadie into the mattress. Flattening her. But even though he willed it, he couldn't seem to move.

Sadie wasn't moving, either, though he felt her heart beat against his chest.

"That…" Sadie said breathlessly from beneath him, "was amazing."

Spence didn't move. "Yeah?" In what way amazing? Amazingly awful?

Sadie's lungs expanded. He could feel her drawing in a deep breath. "Oh, yes! It was wonderful."

His heart skipped a beat. He could almost feel it expand in his chest, as if the weight of the world had suddenly been lifted.

"Mmm." And then she looped her arms around his neck and tugged his face down to plant a kiss on his lips. "The best."

He grinned. He laughed. He couldn't help it. "You think that was good?" he said gruffly. "I'll show you good."

"Now?" Sadie squeaked.

"In a few minutes. How about that?" He rolled off her and drew her against him, marveling at how right she felt in his arms, against his side, as if she belonged there.

"I think I could stand it again in a few minutes," Sadie said after a moment's consideration.

"Good." He settled a hand in her hair. Turned his head to kiss her brow. Could barely believe this was happening. Was he going to wake up and have it all be a dream?

But the night passed…with more lovemaking. Lots of love-making. Spence was determined to show Sadie every kind he could think of. And it wasn't a dream. He was exhausted at dawn. Eyes bloodshot. Body drained. Brain dead.

He didn't care. Sadie agreed it was good. Very very good indeed.

They missed breakfast.

Well, not all of it. But everyone else had finished and was sitting around the lounge drinking cups of tea and coffee when they came in together, looking flushed and distracted and as if they'd spent the night in the honeymoon *bure* doing exactly what honeymooners were expected to do.

And they had.

And they were flushed and distracted because they'd spent the most amazing night together—all of it sleepless—and at dawn they had gone out for a swim.

Spence had suggested it.

"You want to *swim?*" Sadie had stared at him in disbelief. "I'll drown. I feel boneless."

"C'mon." Spence had tugged her hand to pull her up. "It'll be wonderful. You'll see."

He was right. It had been magical. The cool morning air, the water almost warm when they plunged in. They'd romped and played and kissed—and loved.

And then, floating there in the water watching the sun rise out of the ocean, it had become even more wonderful because she'd been floating back against Spence's chest, his arms encircling her, his breath soft against her ear.

Then, once the sky had changed from navy to a stunning mixture of violets and reds and oranges, and finally to the pale yellow and bright blue of morning, they had left the beach and come back to their treehouse *bure*, where they had showered together in the waterfall where Spence had watched her the day before.

Had that been only yesterday? Not even a full twenty-four hours? How was it possible that things had changed so much?

Sadie didn't know. She only knew the joy they had today. And that she felt a little stiff and sore, as if she'd used muscles she was unaccustomed to using. Imagine that, she thought, unable to keep the silly happy grin on her face.

Spence looked equally pleased, though his eyes were decidedly bloodshot and he hadn't shaved because Sadie had decided she liked his stubbly jaw.

She'd urged him not to shave. "Unless you think Mr. Isogawa will object," she'd said, aware that there were other priorities.

"You're more important than Isogawa," Spence had said, rubbing his whiskers lightly against her cheek.

And Sadie couldn't help feeling more important as they came into the lounge, with Spence's arm looped over her shoulders.

One look at them and Sadie was sure everyone knew what they had been doing. She was far too pleased to care. And even when Mr. Isogawa asked politely if they had slept well, she hadn't been able to stop grinning.

"We had a good night," she said. It was the truth, after all, even if they hadn't slept.

"I'll bet you did," Leonie said enviously.

Richard didn't notice, but Marion jumped in and said diplomatically, "It's a wonderful place. John and I enjoyed it, too. Not too hot. Not too cold. Peaceful. And all those lovely gentle waves."

Had she seen them? Sadie wondered, knowing her face was even redder. But Marion didn't give her a knowing grin or wink. Bless her heart.

Cathy beckoned them toward a table with two empty chairs. "Come sit and enjoy your breakfast. It's marvelous. Fresh fruit. Eggs. French toast. Whatever your heart desires, really. We ate too much. Marion and I were just talking about going for a walk while they're all in meetings. Want to come with us?" Her gaze included both Sadie and Leonie.

"Not me," Leonie said promptly. "I'm going to have a massage," she said with a knowing smile. "With Jale."

Jale, the young man who had taken them to their *bure* yesterday, was a definite hunk. And obviously he had more talents than carrying luggage.

Sadie shot a quick glance at Richard to see if she could gauge his reaction to Leonie's plan. But Richard didn't even seem to have heard. He was talking to John, not paying attention to his wife at all.

"I'd love to," Sadie said to Marion and Cathy, "but this isn't just a honeymoon for me. It's work, too. I have to be at the meetings."

Spence hadn't said so, but the truth was, she wanted to go to the meetings.

She wanted to be wherever Spence was, to watch him in action. She wanted to spend the whole day just looking at him, marveling at the fact that finally, after so long, he was really hers and that finally they both knew it.

They hadn't spoken much last night. When the barriers had finally come down it had been too startling, too new, too overwhelming. There had been words, but not many. There would be time later for them.

She had said, "I love you," though.

She'd dared that much, and had held her breath after she'd said it, fearing he would laugh.

He hadn't. He had groaned and kissed her with a desperation that told her he loved her, too. And she had been willing to settle for that. She believed he loved her even if he couldn't yet say it.

But he'd surprised her by pulling back and looking deeply into her eyes and saying, "I love you, too."

She'd blinked, amazed, then exultant. She was confident now that he was the soul mate she had always thought he would be.

Spencer Tyack had always been a guarded man, who charmed others easily, who had many friends—but who loved only a few.

He loved her. He'd said so. And she had no doubt that he would demonstrate that fact again as soon as they had some privacy.

And in the meantime she could watch him. She could take notes as needed, and when they weren't needed she could mentally undress him and rehearse all the things they would do when they were alone.

The very thought made her smile again.

"Newlyweds," Marion chided her, laughing at her dopey smile. "Stop your daydreaming and order your breakfast. You're making me envious, you are."

Sadie felt herself blushing again. But hastily she sat down and one of the waitresses instantly appeared with a menu.

"If you don't see what you want," the waitress told her, smiling, "we will find it for you."

It was hard to imagine anything she might want that was not on the menu. It was as extensive and amazing as Cathy had claimed. And Sadie saw far too many things she wanted because suddenly she was starving.

Finally she settled on a glass of juice, a muffin, an omelet and a cup of tea, though she could probably have eaten a lumberjack-size meal, she'd expended so many calories during the night. But she didn't want everyone to think Spence had married a glutton. She needed to behave properly and with dignity, moderation and decorum—as long as she could be a complete wanton in bed!

A giggle bubbled up.

Cathy and Marion looked at her, shook their heads, still smiling as they sighed. Leonie looked from Sadie to Spence and back again, then turned her head to look daggers at Richard who still didn't notice.

Sadie felt sorry for her and wished she could help, especially since it was due to Leonie's attempt to seduce Spence that she owed her own current happiness. Poor Leonie.

"Ah, I see you are happy this morning." The soft, precisely accented English made Sadie look up to see Mrs. Isogawa standing next to her table.

"I'm very happy," Sadie assured her. "I think this is the most wonderful place on earth!"

"Good place," Mrs. Isogawa agreed. "Happy place. Meet my husband here."

"You did? Here?"

"Yes, yes." Then she glanced over and said something to her husband in Japanese.

"It's true," he agreed. "She was with some friends on a holiday. I was working here. Designing these buildings. Except I couldn't take my eyes off her. I found a way to get introduced to her." His smile widened. "And the rest is, as you say, history."

Sadie was enchanted. It really was a magical place.

"Every year our family comes, too. They will be here later this week. Our sons and daughter and grandchildren. Maybe," he said, "you will come in the future and bring your family, too."

Sadie could get misty and starry-eyed just thinking about it. She glanced over at Spence, but he was listening to something Steve Walker was saying.

"You do not need to come to the meetings today," Mr. Isogawa told her. "If you wish to enjoy the island, my assistant can take notes and give them to you."

"I'd like to come," Sadie replied. "It is my job. But I really want to. I don't usually get to see Spence in this part of his work."

Mr. Isogawa nodded. "Very well. Enjoy your breakfast. We meet in an hour."

Sadie did enjoy her breakfast. And Spence, who was sitting with Richard and Steve, appeared to enjoy his. He was back in business mode, deep in conversation with both of them, barely touching his food as he listened.

But every now and then he glanced up and looked her way. Their gazes would connect and a corner of Spence's mouth would lift.

And Sadie—remembering last night and thinking of all the nights to come—felt joy fill her heart again.

The guys had been on him the minute he and Sadie had reached the dining area, Richard with a sheaf of papers, Steve and John with a host of questions.

If he'd been worried that they would wonder what he was up to all night, he needn't have bothered. This morning they were all too absorbed in things they wanted to talk about regarding Nanumi.

Nanumi. *Remember*, Sadie had said it meant. And now Spence felt he had a right to do just that. The instant he had borne her back onto the bed and wrapped her in his arms, he'd had the sense that he'd been here before. All the kaleidoscopic bits of memory—sounds, shapes, touches, feelings—that he'd made himself blot out, came tumbling back. And as he'd made love with Sadie last night, he had felt as if he were assembling pieces of a puzzle he'd put together before. He heard echoes of words he'd heard before and feelings he already knew.

It was fresh—and yet it was oddly familiar, too.

Mostly it was completely right.

In their lovemaking Spence recognized a feeling he'd never experienced before that single night four years ago—a feeling he hadn't felt since. He had lost it without even realizing he'd had it—in Sadie's arms he found again the feeling of being welcome, of finally, after a lifetime of searching, finding the place where he belonged.

With Sadie.

The notion still had the power to stun him when he thought about it too long. It was like staring into the sun. Brilliant but impossible. And yet—

Sadie loved him.

She'd said so. Fervently. Eagerly. Even desperately, or so it appeared.

Pretty much like he loved her.

He'd even told her. And that had stunned him, too. Spence could never remember having said the words to anyone in his entire life. But with Sadie, the words had come out unbidden.

She had said them first, and maybe he'd been responding to that.

But he didn't think so. He thought he really loved her—and had for a very long time.

That surprised him, too. Of course he had always liked Sadie, even as a knobby-kneed, gap-toothed five-year-old, when she'd tagged after him and Danny all those years ago. As he watched her grow up, he'd admired her determination, her intelligence, her talents.

He'd certainly appreciated her help when she'd first come to work for him. They'd had a great time. He'd missed her desperately while she was away at college in California—because she had been such an asset to his business, he'd thought then. And for that reason, he assured himself, he had done whatever he'd needed to do to make sure she'd come back afterward.

It was the truth.

But not the whole truth.

Spence understood that now. For years he understood there had been more to his relationship with Sadie Morrissey than he'd been willing to admit. Clear back when she'd been in high school, there had been those early twinges of sexual attraction, that awareness of her curves and mile-long legs, of the feminine attributes that changed her from the knobby-kneed, gap-toothed kid to a delectable, appealing young woman.

A young woman far too good for him. And if his own good sense hadn't prevented him from acting on his feelings, Danny's fierce "Leave her alone. You've got nothing to offer her," took care of any inclinations he'd had. At least until the trauma of Emily's defection had jolted him so badly that his instincts had taken over.

Then he'd dared ask a question buried so deep he hadn't dared to even think it. He'd done what his heart had desired. He'd married Sadie.

And ruined it all again the next day.

But he hadn't been able to ruin it forever. Quite by accident he'd been given a second chance. And he was glad. More than glad. Over the moon.

Last night Sadie had made him feel alive, whole. She'd made him feel like no one had ever made him feel in his life.

She'd made him feel loved—something Spence had always recognized more by experience of its absence than its presence in his life.

Other people loved. Other families. Not his.

But none of it mattered now because Sadie loved him. She'd shown him that love last night. All night. And this morning while he was supposed to be paying attention to Richard and Steve, he kept glancing over at Sadie during breakfast. And she glanced back, grinning all over her face.

Spence grinned, too, because never in his life had he felt like this.

He was the same Spencer Tyack he had always been. The same wrong-side-of-the-tracks son of down-and-out parents who had spent his life scrabbling to try to become someone—and had.

But frankly he felt reborn. Alive. Nothing he had earned or achieved or become came close to describing the gift Sadie had given him with her love.

"…listening to a word I've said?" Richard Carstairs's rough voice penetrated the blissful fog that clouded Spence's brain.

Spence dragged his attention back briefly from far more interesting contemplations. "What? Yes, of course I'm listening."

But he couldn't seem to focus on anyone but Sadie. She'd finished her breakfast. Where had she gone?

His gaze didn't stop moving until he found her out on the deck, the breeze lifting her hair, the late-morning sunlight kissing her cheeks. They looked redder than usual. Probably his fault. Whisker burn had been the last thing on his mind last night. And this morning she hadn't wanted him to shave.

"I like it," she'd said, rubbing her palm over his cheek. "Very sexy." He was glad she liked it.

"—build some stables as well," Richard said. "Don't you agree?"

"Mmm."

"Let the man eat his breakfast," Steve said gruffly. "He'll listen to you soon enough."

Richard grumbled, but put his sheaf of papers away, then looked around absently. "Where's Leonie?"

"Don't know." Don't care, Spence thought. But feeling generous—and in fact feeling as if he owed Leonie something for having inadvertently prompted him to bring Sadie along, he said to Richard, "You ought to find her. See if she's having a good time. Go for a swim with her."

"A swim?" Richard looked aghast.

"It's what Isogawa wanted us to have this week for," Spence

reminded him with the zeal of the converted. "Remembering what's important. Reconnecting with family."

Richard shook his head. "Leonie's my wife, not my family."

Spence didn't see the difference, but he was no expert. "Just a thought," he said mildly.

Richard grunted and went back to his papers.

Sadie spent the two hours before lunch and two hours after attending the meetings, taking copious notes—and Spence-watching. And if it was possible to find more reasons to love the man she'd married four years ago, Sadie did it that afternoon.

It had been a long time since she'd seen Spence at work other than in the office in Butte working one-on-one with her. But today she saw him working with people, listening to ideas, visualizing, synthesizing, concretizing. He took a group of men with diverse agendas and individual concerns and brought them to a group agreement.

It wasn't all settled yet, of course. The deal wasn't done. But he had connected with Mr. Isogawa. The respect between them was clear. And his rapport with the others was also there. When Richard seemed about to go off on a tangent, Spence tactfully and speedily redirected his focus. When John got bogged down in the details, Spence took him back to the big picture. He had a way with words and a way with people that gave them confidence and helped them zero in on the program.

"You were spectacular," she told him after when the meeting broke up for the afternoon.

He grinned, all boyish enthusiasm. "You're prejudiced," he told her.

"But that doesn't mean I'm wrong." And then, because she dared now show her feelings, she raised up on tiptoe and kissed him.

He kissed her back, a warm, possessive kiss. And when all

the men gave them a round of applause and a couple of cheers, he slung an arm around her shoulder and said, "If you'll excuse us, gentlemen, my wife and I have things to discuss."

They "discussed" for the rest of the afternoon. They made love in their bed and under the waterfall in their private outdoor spa. It was far more wickedly wonderful and erotic than Sadie had ever dared imagine.

Spence left her, boneless and replete, then had to get dressed to meet Richard and Mr. Isogawa to look at the place where Richard had suggested they might want to put in some stables.

"You don't mind?" he said.

"Of course not. It's what you're here for."

He bent over her on the bed and kissed her with lazy thoroughness. "Want to go for a swim tonight?"

"A swim?" She grinned.

"And all that that entails."

"Love to. Love you," she said, and smiled as she watched him stuff his feet into his flip-flops and head out the door.

Sadie took another shower after he left. Then she dressed and went for a walk on the beach.

Leonie was standing near a group of beach chairs, talking with Jale. He was smiling while she batted her lashes at him and ran a hand down his arm. When she saw Sadie, she waved him off, and, looking almost relieved, he hurried away.

"Just arranging another massage," Leonie explained as Sadie came up. "He's very good. Sure you don't want one?"

Sadie wasn't sure how much to read into the "very good" but she did know the answer to the question. "No, thanks."

Leonie sat down on a beach towel and stretched her legs out, wiggling her toes. "I suppose you don't need anyone else with his hands on you." She flicked Sadie a sideways glance.

"Besides Spence, you mean? No."

"He's obviously nuts about you."

A day ago Sadie wouldn't have believed it. Now she said, "The feeling is mutual."

"I can tell." There was a grudging envy in Leonie's tone.

Sadie let it go. "Are you enjoying yourself?" she asked.

"What do you think?"

Oops. Wrong question.

"I know how much you wanted to come and—" Sadie began to back pedal.

"Did Spence tell you about Barcelona?"

Sadie's gaze jerked over to meet the other woman's. The color was high in Leonie's cheeks, but she didn't look away. Nor did Sadie. At least they weren't going to have to pretend it hadn't happened. She nodded. "Yes."

"Figures." Leonie gave a bitter half laugh. "When I saw you with him yesterday morning at the airport in Nadi, when he said you were married, I thought maybe he was pretending—to avoid me, you know? To make sure Richard didn't find out and ruin the deal." She shook her head. "How's that for egocentric?"

Sadie hoped the question was rhetorical.

"Spence and I have actually been together for a long time," she said. "We just thought we shouldn't make an issue of it. You know, during work."

"I understand." Leonie grimaced. "Lucky you. I envy you. Oh, not about Spence." She paused. "Well, to be honest, yes, about Spence. He's dynamite. But it's more that he actually pays attention to you."

Unlike Richard.

Sadie understood. From what she'd seen, Richard barely seemed to register that his wife was there.

"Was that why you went to, um, Spence's...in Barcelona?" she asked, not quite finding the words to say it. "The reason for the massages? And Jale?"

Leonie nodded grimly. "I keep hoping Richard will wake up!"

"By making him jealous?"

"Why not? I want him to notice me… Remember that I'm his wife. How else can I wake him up?"

"Tell him?" It was more a question than a suggestion. God knew Sadie was the last person who should be giving advice about how to improve a marriage.

"Tell him I want a baby?"

"A baby?" Sadie stared at Leonie. "Do you?"

The leap from "notice me" to "want a baby" was substantial.

"I do, yes. I know Richard already has grown children. I know he thinks he's finished with all that. But I'm not! I love him. I want a child with him. A family. Don't you?"

"Yes, of course we do." Sadie didn't have to think an instant about that. She'd been dreaming about a family with Spence since she'd been old enough to know how babies were made. She already had names picked out for their children, though she supposed she'd allow him some input.

"But I didn't realize you did. Doesn't Richard?"

"We haven't discussed it," Leonie admitted. Then she got a mulish expression on her face. "How could we? He barely acts like I'm alive. It's weird, you know. He was all over me before we got married. I got complete attention. Once he had the ring on my finger, he went right back to work. Marrying me was like doing a deal. The thrill of the hunt. Once he got me, he wasn't interested anymore."

"Maybe you should tell him how you feel. Maybe he thinks you don't want kids."

"Maybe he's never even considered it!"

"You'll never know until you try."

"I guess I just hoped he'd realize…"

"Read your mind?" Sadie smiled.

Leonie shrugged. "Something like that."

"Trust me," Sadie said with feeling. "Speaking from experience. It doesn't work. You have to say the words."

Leonie sighed, then picked up a fistful of sand and let it trickle out through her fingers. Then she tipped her head to the side and looked at Sadie. "You are so lucky," she murmured. "Do you have any idea how lucky?"

And Sadie, thinking back over the past four years in limbo and the last night in Spence's arms, dug her toes into the warm sand and felt the kiss of the sun on her face and could only nod and smile.

"Yes," she said softly. "Yes, I do."

CHAPTER NINE

"I TALKED to Leonie this afternoon." Sadie was lying on her side in bed, tracing a line down the center of Spence's bare chest, then following it with her lips.

"Mmm." It was an acknowledgment that he heard her, but his attention was clearly elsewhere. He shifted as her mouth moved lower, then held still, sucking in his breath.

"You're very tense," Sadie murmured, teasing his navel with her tongue, then moving lower still.

"Not tense," Spence muttered. "Wrung out."

"But obviously not unwilling to continue." Sadie grinned and kept on tracing, touching, teasing.

They had gone back to their room after dinner, a memorable meal, succulent pork and locally grown vegetables cooked in a *lovo*, or Fijian earth oven. But while almost everyone else had taken Mr. Isogawa up on his offer of drinks in the bar afterward, Spence had said he and Sadie needed to go over some papers.

"Go over some papers?" Sadie had said doubtfully,

Spence had waited until they were out of earshot. Then he'd grinned. "We'll put them under the bed."

She didn't know if they were under there or not. She and Spence had been in the bed—except when they'd been in the waterfall shower—for most of the rest of the evening.

Their lovemaking had been by turns heated and passionate,

then leisurely and frolicksome. It was everything Sadie could ever have wanted it to be. It spoke of the closeness, the trust and the intimacy that she and Spence had achieved.

And in the joy of their love, she remembered Leonie's unhappy face.

"You were right," she said now, looking up between kisses. "She did intend to seduce you."

Spence jerked halfway up, weight resting on his elbows. "She told you that?" He looked appalled.

Sadie moved her shoulders. "She did, actually. She thinks you're gorgeous," she added with a grin. "But it was really more about Richard. She was trying to make him jealous. He didn't notice, apparently."

"And thank God for that," Spence said dryly. "Or this whole thing would have fallen through. It's too bad, though, if she really does care," he reflected. "Richard tends to get pretty single-minded at times." He settled back down, the fingers of one hand playing in Sadie's hair, making her scalp tingle.

She bent her head and continued her exploratory kissing. "At one time, apparently, he was single-minded about pursuing her. Like she was some sort of trophy. And then when he got her, he forgot her." She nipped his belly.

Spence's fingers clenched in her curls. "She's not exactly destitute. She's getting something out of the marriage," he pointed out. "World travel. A fantastic house. Three fantastic houses, for that matter. One in Florida, one in England, one in Costa Rica. She wouldn't be cavorting around Fiji now if it weren't for Richard."

"I don't think it's Fiji Leonie cares about. Or the fantastic houses. It's her marriage. It's Richard. She loves him."

"She's got a damn funny way of showing it, then. Why doesn't she just say so?"

"That's what I told her." Sadie eased her way down and let

her fingers walk along his thighs, first one and then the other, then dipping between them and making him squirm.

"Asking for trouble," Spence muttered.

"No. A baby," Sadie said, kissing him exactly where she'd been aiming for all along.

Spence jerked. *"What?"*

"Leonie," Sadie said, breathing on him, tasting him, making him gasp, "wants a baby."

Spence was strangling. "Forget babies! I don't care what Leonie wants! I want you!" Hastily he sheathed himself to protect her, then hauled her up to straddle him and thrust to meet her—to make them one once more.

And Sadie met him eagerly, delighting in the way they moved together, rocked together, loved together. Shattered together.

"I love you," she breathed as she collapsed on top of him. Her head rested on his chest. His heart thundered in her ear. She turned her face to press a kiss there, then she lifted her head and smiled tenderly up at him. "Sometime soon maybe we'll have a baby, too."

He didn't respond. He just lay there with his fingers threaded through her hair, relishing its silken softness. He turned his head and pressed a kiss against her cheek. "I love you, too," he whispered and wrapped his arms around her, holding her close while she dozed. He still wanted her and it wasn't that long before his body was ready again to love her.

He ran his hands down her back, began to kiss her.

She squirmed against him, as eager as he was to love again.

He smiled. "I think," Spence whispered against her ear, "that life is plenty full enough as it is."

"Richard thought he was hearing things," Leonie reported Friday morning.

They were on the beach while the men were tidying up the last details of the Nanumi agreement.

Sadie had wondered since their conversation earlier in the week, but she hadn't wanted to ask. And nothing in Leonie's demeanor before today had given her any reason to hope. But this morning the other woman's eyes were wide and there was a light in them that Sadie had never seen before.

"You told him?"

"Well, I had to get his attention first. I tried talking, but he kept right on working away on his damned laptop. So after three tries, I finally grabbed it and threatened to stomp it into oblivion if he didn't listen."

Now it was Sadie who was wide-eyed. "You didn't!"

"Well, I didn't stomp it, but I could have," Leonie admitted. "I may not be trying to seduce Spence anymore, but I still believe in dramatic gestures. I just had to find one that got his attention. That did."

Sadie was impressed. "I'll bet. So what did he say?"

"He was surprised. Stunned, really. I guess we never did talk enough before we got married. It was very rush-rush. I told you, he acted like he had to win me. And he did. But he thought I'd married him for his money, and that was all. The idiot didn't realize I really loved him!" Leonie shook her head and made a sound that was somewhere between a laugh and a sob.

Sadie was amazed. "And now he does?"

"He's…working on it. I think I gave him something to think about."

Sadie just bet she had. "And the baby? What did he think about that?"

"He couldn't believe I meant it. He thought he was too old. That *I* would think he was too old. I told him he wasn't the one who'd be pregnant! And then he wondered what his kids would think. I said, 'Ask them,' and that surprised him, too."

"That you would offer to let them voice an opinion?"

"I suppose. I think he thinks they won't approve. I think he thinks they don't approve of his marrying me. But that's not their decision. It's his, though they could certainly have told him if they wanted to. And they won't make this decision, either. But why shouldn't he ask if he wants to know how they feel?"

It seemed like eminently good sense to Sadie. And she said so.

Leonie smiled. "I hope so. We'll see. He's told me a hundred times what a big step it is. He says I should take a good look at the Isogawas' grandchildren tomorrow and see if I really want all that hassle. But he's not saying no. He's actually interested. Tempted, I think. Mostly, though, he knows I really love him now. And—" she threw her arms around Sadie and gave her a crushing hug "—we owe it all to you!"

"She says she owes it all to me," Sadie reported, grinning.

"Huh? Who owes what?" Spence was distracted, she could tell. He'd been eager to wrap her in his arms as soon as he'd found her on the beach. And he'd spirited her away from Leonie without a backward glance. Something was on his mind.

"I said, Leonie and Richard are talking to each other," she repeated patiently while they walked up to their *bure*. "He's actually listening to her. They're communicating! They might have a baby! And she says she owes it all to me." She was sure Spence would appreciate the irony of it.

But he just shook his head. "The woman's nuts."

Well, he'd had a hard day. While Sadie had only attended the morning meetings, he'd been tied up all afternoon hammering out the last of the details so that the new resort consortium was now a done deal. So he could be forgiven not caring one way or another about Leonie's family issues.

"You must be relieved that it's over," Sadie said as they climbed the steps up to the treehouse porch. Once there she reached up to knead the taut muscles of his shoulders and back.

Spence sighed. "Yeah." He let her hands work their magic for a few moments, then straightened. "I was thinking we ought to go home."

"Home?" Sadie's hands stilled.

"We can't stay here forever. It's paradise, yes. But the work's done."

"But the week isn't. Mr. Isogawa expects us to be here. Besides, tomorrow's family day." And she'd been looking forward to that.

Spence shrugged. "Isogawa's family."

"And we want to meet them. They come back every year— all of them—Mr. and Mrs. Isogawa, their kids and grandkids. It's what Nanumi is all about. It's what we've worked on all week."

Spence's jaw tightened briefly. But then he shrugged. "Fine. If you want to stay, we'll stay." He walked into the room and fell on the bed face down. His eyes shut.

Sadie sat down next to him and began rubbing his back again. "All the adrenaline's gone, isn't it?"

He rolled over and grabbed her, pulling her down on top of him. "Don't you believe it!"

He was still sound asleep when she awoke the next morning.

And no wonder, Sadie thought. He'd kept them up most of the night. He had loved her eagerly, urgently, almost desperately, in a way that reminded her of their wedding night four years ago.

But it wasn't like that, Sadie was sure, because there was no forgetting what had happened between them here.

It was nearly eight. She'd promised to meet the Isogawas and their family for breakfast at nine. That gave her time for a lei-surely shower—provided Spence didn't join her—before she had to be there. She wouldn't have minded at all if he had joined her. But she knew he was exhausted.

She looked at him now, her heart full to bursting at the love she felt for this man. She reached out and brushed a hand lightly over his tousled hair. He didn't stir. She leaned down and kissed his stubbled cheek. He sighed and smiled slightly, but he didn't wake.

She took her shower, then dried her hair and combed it, taking more care than she had all week so she would be presentable for meeting the Isogawa family. When she left at five minutes to nine, Spence still hadn't moved.

The sound of children's laughter woke him. Startled him.

For a moment Spence didn't know where he was. Then he opened his eyes and remembered. Family day.

Talk about a foreign experience.

He lay there considering the best way to avoid the whole thing, when there was a knock on the *bure* door. He frowned because in the entire week, no one had come knocking. Everyone had respected his and Sadie's privacy. But maybe Sadie had sent a messenger to see if he was ever getting up.

He pulled on a pair of shorts and opened the door, blinked when he didn't see anyone, then realized the knocker barely came up to his chest.

Two girls and three boys were standing there, hopping and jigging from one foot to the other.

"We've never seen a tree house this big. You live here?" The tallest boy asked him, eyes wide. He sounded like a Kiwi and looked like Steve, so Spence had a pretty good idea who he was.

"This week I do," he replied, as they craned their necks and peered past him into the room. Their eagerness reminded him of his own youthful curiosity. "Want to have a look around?"

Did they? He was practically trampled in the rush to explore. They were fascinated by the way the *bure* was built around the branches, that one of them was so big that it could be used as a "window seat." They were delighted with the private waterfall.

"Can we go in it?" the redheaded girl asked.

He shrugged. "Be my guests." And as they danced and

hopped and skittered through it, laughing all the while, Spence laughed, too. He told them his name and found out theirs. The biggest boy, Geoff, and the littlest, Justin, belonged to Steve and Cathy. The middle one was Keefe Ten Eyk. The redheaded girl was his sister, Katie, and the other was Mai, the Isogawas' granddaughter. She didn't speak English but the language barrier wasn't slowing them down any.

"This is amaaaazing," Keefe said. "I could live here my whole life!"

"Which is soon to end," came a voice from the door. And a very stern Marion appeared. "You know better than to bother the guests."

"We asked," Katie said. "Politely."

All the rest of the kids nodded in agreement.

"He said be his guest," Justin piped up. "Didn't you?" He looked at Spence for confirmation.

"Absolutely," Spence agreed.

"They didn't wake you?" Marion was still looking worried. "Sadie said you were exhausted, that you needed your sleep."

"I was awake. I was just coming down for a swim."

Justin grabbed one of his hands, and Mai shyly took the other. "C'mon, then."

"Leave Mr. Tyack alone," Marion said. "Out now. All of you. And say thank you for his kindness at letting you interrupt his life."

"They didn't. They were fine." And Spence took the hands of the kids who had dropped his and led them out the door and down the steps. "Hit the beach." He swung their hands up, and when he let go they all took off running, yelling whooping—even Mai who couldn't possibly have understood.

Marion lingered beside him. "Crazy children. They think they've been turned loose on Swiss Family Robinson's island. Thank you. I'm sorry they bothered you."

"It's all right," Spence said again. "They're fine."

"Glad you feel that way," Marion said, then patted him on the arm. When he raised a quizzical brow, she turned and nodded toward the group coming down from the lodge.

The group included both the elder Isogawas, a younger couple Spence presumed were their children, with two more grandchildren much smaller than Mai.

A little boy just learning to walk was holding on to Richard on one side and Leonie on the other while he took staggering steps toward the beach and Richard and Leonie laughed and made encouraging noises.

The other child was nestled in Sadie's arms.

"She's in her element now," Marion said, watching Sadie with a smile on her face.

And Spence, watching, had to agree.

He'd always known she'd doted on Edward, Martha and Theo's little boy. It was a woman thing, he figured, because every time Martha brought him in, Sadie scooped the little boy up and danced him around the office, blew kisses on his belly, made him laugh and told him nursery rhymes.

"She'll be a good mother," Marion assured him.

"Yeah." She would.

Sadie had enjoyed all the other days—and of course she'd loved the nights—but family day was the best.

She got to play with the Isogawas' grandchildren. She got to watch Spence playing with the bigger kids. She got to imagine what it would be like when they had their own children someday, even though she knew she shocked everyone when Leonie had asked her how many children she wanted and she said, "Eight."

"Ha!" John Ten Eyk had laughed.

And Marion had shuddered and said, "Rather you than me!"

"Sadie could handle them," Cathy said firmly.

But the look on Spence's face was so appalled she'd hastened to reassure him. "I don't really want eight," she said quickly. "I know how much work kids are now. So I think maybe three or four would be wonderful. Even one or two. Whatever we get, I guess. And if we don't get any we can adopt."

Something was wrong. Sadie could tell.

When the kids went to eat dinner with their parents, she and Spence ate with Richard and Leonie, who suddenly were acting more like newlyweds than she and Spence were. Leonie was bubbling with enthusiasm as they talked about the Isogawas' grandchildren.

Far from putting her off having children, the day had whetted her appetite. And Richard didn't seem to be averse to the idea.

"My kids—my *old* kids," he corrected himself, "will just have to get used to it if I have another one. It's not like they're teenagers embarrassed by everything Dad does."

"Of course not," Sadie said. "Tony Hunt, one of the artists in Spence's art co-op became a father again in his fifties three years ago. His son is his grandson's best friend. Right?" She looked at Spence.

"Yeah." He shoved a delicious piece of *lovo*-cooked pork around on his plate. He didn't say anything else.

Sadie studied him in silence during the meal. He had got more sun today than the other days. There had been no meetings, just fun and games on the beach. Maybe he'd got too much sun. Maybe he didn't feel well.

"I think," she said when she finished her own meal, "that I'd like to call it a night. I've got a lot of packing to do before our flight leaves in the morning. Do you want to come?" she asked her husband. "Or do you want to stay and visit some more?"

He shoved back his chair and stood. "I'll come."

They said goodbye to the Carstairs. Richard shook hands heartily. Leonie hugged both her and Spence hard and whispered, "You guys are the best. We have a baby, we'll name it after one of you."

Sadie laughed. "I think you should discuss that with Richard first."

They wished everyone else goodbye, too. Their plane was leaving early in the morning. The Carstairs were staying another week for some determined "together time." And both New Zealand couples had a later flight back to Nadi and then home.

The Isogawas bowed then hugged Sadie, probably because she hugged them first. "I know it's probably not at all the proper thing to do," she told them. "But this has been the most wonderful week of my life. So thank you. Thank you!"

"Thank *you* for everything, too," Mr. Isogawa said. "You are part of Nanumi now. You will come back." And then he bowed and shook Spence's hand. "It is not goodbye. It is a new beginning for all of us. I thank you. I look forward to seeing you soon on Nanumi."

Spence bowed and shook hands, too. He said thank you as well, his voice quiet and grave. He bowed to Mrs. Isogawa. He said good night to everyone else and then he walked out into the star-washed night with Sadie.

He held her arm so that she didn't stumble as they walked down the plankway. He didn't speak. Neither did she. She was drinking in the beauty, savoring the memories, knowing she would take them out and replay them in her mind over and over again.

Spence opened the door to their *bure* and held it for her. She stepped past him inside, then turned and wrapped him tight in her arms. For a second he stiffened. But then his arms came hard around her and he just hung on.

"It was wonderful," Sadie said. "It *is* wonderful."

He gave her a little squeeze and rested his cheek against her hair. He just stood there. Didn't let go. Until Sadie finally loosed her arms and took half a step away to look up into his eyes.

"What's wrong?"

"Nothing." He swallowed. "I'm fine. I—" He stopped, took a breath, then started again. He looked pale now and there were lines of strain around his mouth. "What you said about kids…"

Sadie laughed. "I was kidding! Don't worry. We won't have eight."

"No, we won't."

"But however many we have, I want them all to look like you."

"No."

"Yes. I've had a thing for you forever. For my whole life. And I can't imagine anything more wonderful that lots of dark-haired little rascals just like you."

Spence shook his head. "No. I can't."

"What?" Sadie stared at him, stunned. "Can't what?"

"Won't," he corrected. "Have kids. I don't want any kids at all."

CHAPTER TEN

"I DON'T want kids." He repeated the words again. "I won't have any."

And Sadie could see by the way he paced and by the ferocity with which he cracked his knuckles that, unlike her, he wasn't joking.

"Well, we might not have any," she said, taken aback by both the sentiment and the ferocity.

"But then you want to adopt!"

"What's wrong with adoption?"

"Nothing. Nothing at all!" Another knuckle crack. "It's great. Fine. Terrific. For someone else. No kids, Sadie. I can't do it."

"But—"

"I can't. I won't be responsible for giving a kid the kind of rotten childhood I had!"

"Oh, for heaven's sake. Is that what you're worried about? It won't be that kind of childhood!"

"How do you know?"

"I just know," she said stubbornly. "How can you even think that?"

"Because I lived it, damn it. It's hell—and it's what I know. I can't do it. I won't! No kids. I made up my mind years ago."

"Spence—"

He folded his arms across his chest. "No."

She wanted to argue. She wanted to pound on his thick skull and tell him to stop being an idiot.

But there was no arguing with Spence when he got bull-headed like this. What made him a great developer was his ability to be flexible, to see options where others saw only one outcome.

But he wasn't seeing any other options now. He saw only one—the life he'd had.

"Spence," she began, softening her voice, gentling, trying to get past the wall he'd built. But he shook his head.

"That's the way it's going to be, Sadie. No kids. Period."

Stubborn jackass. Mule-headed fool. She could go through a whole barnyard of obstinacy if he kept this up.

"You can visit all the kids you want. I'll never stop you."

"Oh, thank you very much." Her voice was sharper now. Gentleness wasn't going to begin to penetrate the steel he'd wrapped around his heart. "How very nice of you."

"I know you like kids and—"

"*You* like kids! That wasn't you out there today, playing with them? Jumping around in the water with them? Letting Justin climb all over you?"

"Of course I like them. But that doesn't mean I intend to raise them!"

"You can't just unilaterally lay down edicts like that."

"Of course I can. I just did."

"Spence—"

"No. And I'm not going to change my mind. Sorry. If it mattered so much, you should have asked. Emily knew. Dena knew. They were fine with it."

"Well, I'm not. And you never told me."

"I'm telling you now." Their gazes met, dueled.

"Not good enough."

He shook his head. "Sorry. That's the way it is." And

abruptly he turned away. He strode over to the closet and began packing, stuffing things in his suitcase, keeping his back to her. His movements were jerky, angry. There was none of the fluid ease she usually associated with the way Spence moved. Nothing he'd said since they'd come into the room was what she would have associated with Spence, either.

It wasn't like Spence to be dogmatic. He knew what he wanted, and he went after it.

But he'd always wanted her to argue. And he'd always listened.

"Spence," she tried again. "You need to be logical about this. You need to think clearly before you make hard-and-fast pronouncements like that."

He turned, leveling his gaze on her. "I have thought, damn it. What the hell do you think I spent my life doing?"

"I—"

"No, it's you who are going to have to be logical, who are going to have to think clearly and make a decision. Because if you want kids, Sadie—one kid or eight kids or 153 kids—you don't want to be married to me! You want a divorce."

She stared, openmouthed. Stunned.

Divorce? He was talking divorce? Again? After the most beautiful week of their lives?

"Divorce," he repeated, in case she hadn't heard him the first time he'd dropped the word like a granite boulder into the silence of the room. "Think about it."

Then he banged down the lid of his suitcase and stalked into the bathroom. The door shut. The shower turned on.

No waterfall shower together tonight, then. No eager lovemaking. No steamy passion.

Well, there had been passion. But it hadn't been steamy. It had been angry. Passionate anger. Irrational anger. Irrational thoughts.

Because of some fear of giving their children the same sort

of childhood he'd had. No chance of that! It didn't make sense. He had to realize that. Had to.

But she didn't think he did. Sadie sat down on the bed, feeling cold and sick as the realization that he really believed that sank in.

Don't overreact, she cautioned herself. *That's what he's doing. Calm down. Take it easy.*

So she took a deep steadying breath and made herself get up and start to pack. Taking things out of drawers and off hangers was mechanical and mindless, but somehow calming. And packing the various clothes she'd worn during the week made her recall the occasions when she'd worn them. Good times all. And even better times when they had come back to the *bure* and Spence had taken them off her. To make love to her. To share his body, heart and soul with her.

But he'd never shared this.

How could he not want children?

He was so good with them. And they had loved him.

They'd clambered all over him today. And Spence had instinctively known how to treat each of them. He'd roughhoused with Justin and Keefe, had listened intently to Geoff's opinions, had charmed Katie and had no doubt made a lifelong devotee out of Mai by picking her for his team when they'd played ball.

How could he not want to have the chance to do that for children of his own?

She didn't know. Didn't understand. All she could think was that he would come to his senses. He had to come to his senses.

Had to.

He'd known she would be shocked. He'd known she wouldn't be happy. And he knew that marrying her without having told her wasn't fair.

Of course, the fact that he thought he'd immediately

divorced her was somewhat of an excuse! He stood under the shower, letting steaming hot water pour over his head and down his body and tried to think.

It wasn't a big secret. He had told Emily, just as he'd told Sadie he had. Not that it had mattered, when she hadn't even bothered to show up for their wedding. There might have been significant things on which they differed—and there must have been, since she hadn't turned up—but his "no kids" edict hadn't been one of them.

He had been clear on the "no kids" count with Dena, too.

She'd been relieved to hear it. A consummate career woman with, as she put it, "not a single maternal bone in her body," Dena had broken off a relationship to Bahamian investor Carson Sawyer when he decided he wanted a family. She knew she didn't.

So she had been delighted when Spence had said he had no interest in one either. "I knew it," she'd said. "I knew we were right for each other."

But then Sadie had intervened. When she'd shown up at the courthouse with the news that she was still his wife, she'd thrown everybody's plans out of whack.

She'd also given him the most beautiful joyous week he'd ever known.

He couldn't forget that. Never wanted to.

But he couldn't lead her on, either. He couldn't pretend to want a future he had no intention of pursuing. He supposed he should have told her the day they'd been making love and she'd told him about Leonie wanting a baby.

But how?

Was he supposed to say, "Stop driving me madly insane with what you're doing for a minute so I can tell you I don't want children?" And then what? Tell her to go ahead and wring him out? Because that's exactly what she'd been doing.

And after, when she'd said she hoped they would have a baby someday, too, he couldn't bring himself to spoil the moment.

So, all right, he was a selfish bastard. An emotional coward. But at least he was honest. She had to give him that.

He shut off the shower and stood still in the stall, shivering. Cold clear through.

He didn't want to hurt her. He hated to hurt her. He loved her, damn it. But he'd had to tell her. He couldn't let her go on dreaming about some brood of children they were going to have.

She'd get over it. She was an adult, after all.

What if they couldn't have had children? Lots of couples couldn't. Would she hate him then? Would she love him less?

No. Not and still be Sadie. He knew it. He believed in the power of her love to the depths of his being.

She just needed time to adjust. To understand. He needed to give her time. Space. He needed to show her that he loved her—and then she would.

There were different kinds of silence. Sadie knew that. But she'd never experienced it so vividly as that night.

Spence came out of the shower, a *sula* wrapped around his waist, his chest still damp, his hair in wet spikes. He looked at her, his expression unreadable, then he turned away to stow his leather dopp kit in his suitcase. He didn't say a word.

Neither did Sadie.

She didn't know what to say. Everything that occurred to her would, she imagined, make matters worse. She knew Spence—or thought she did—well enough to know that backing him into a corner wasn't going to get him to change his mind. And pretending to give in to his demand wasn't going to help, either. She could hardly just smile and blithely say, "No problem."

It was a problem. That was the truth.

"Shall I set the alarm clock?" The question was very polite. Very civil. Very remote.

"Probably a good idea," she answered in a like tone. "We wouldn't want to miss the plane."

"Since we're going to be the only ones on it, I imagine they'll wait." He didn't smile.

They'd have laughed about that yesterday. Today she just nodded. "Do what you want, then."

He opened his mouth, as if he were going to tell her what he wanted. Or tell her something, at least. But he must have thought better of it because he closed his mouth again. His lips pressed into a thin hard line. He didn't speak.

He set the alarm and lay down on the bed, eyes hooded but watching her.

Another night she would have gone straight to him. She would have crawled onto the bed beside him and he would have wrapped her in his arms and started them down the path to bliss. Tonight, as he folded his arms under his head and watched her, she couldn't do it.

"I'll take a shower, then," she said tonelessly. And, plucking her nightgown off the hook, she disappeared into the bathroom just as he had. She shut the door.

She would have loved one last shower in the waterfall outside. She would have loved to have shared it with Spence. But there was no easiness between them now. No sense of togetherness. No "us" any longer.

And while she knew, if she did shower out there, that he would be watching her, she didn't feel like being on display. She wanted a shower in privacy, where if she cried—no, make that *when* she cried—Spence would never know.

Her eyes were so bloodshot when she came out, though, that if he'd been able to see her, he certainly would have known.

But when she returned, the overhead light had been turned

off. He had left on one dim light next to her side of the bed. He was still there, but lying on his side—turned away from hers.

Was he awake? She didn't know.

He didn't say a word.

In the silence Sadie shut out the light, then slid into bed beside him. It felt like Kansas again. Maybe Texas.

No. More like Alaska. Big and wide. And cold.

Her throat ached from crying. Not because she couldn't have her way. But because he'd cut off all dialogue. He'd made a unilateral decision based solely on memories she couldn't share. And then he'd retreated behind the wall of a childhood she couldn't change.

She sucked in a sharp breath and pressed her fist against her mouth to keep from making noise. But he heard it and rolled over at once.

"Don't cry, for God's sake!" His voice was as harsh and pained as her heart.

"I'll cry if I want to, you ass," she retorted, and did exactly that.

"Oh, hell." He reached for her then, hauling her into his arms, holding her, kissing her. "It'll be all right," he promised. "Shh. I'm sorry."

She hiccupped and tried to stop. But the feel of his arms around her, of his care and his concern undid her. It was so stupid. *He* was so stupid! How could he deny this part of himself to children he could love?

"Don't," he whispered urgently. "Sadie. Please. Stop." He kissed her then, in desperation, no doubt. How else could a guy shut up a crying woman? The kiss was urgent, hungry. In it was so much of everything she loved about Spence, she couldn't help but respond.

She kissed him back, wrapped herself around him, as desperate for him as he was for her. Their coupling was silent but for ragged gasps and breathing. It was fierce, demanding.

But in the end, instead of fulfilled and complete as he rolled off her and lay there staring silently at the ceiling, mostly she felt empty and lost.

She smiled the next morning. She talked to him. Yes, there was still a certain reserve there, a little strain, maybe a hint of dullness in her eyes. He didn't blame her. He knew she was upset. But it was early days yet.

She would get used to it.

He just needed to be patient.

Their trip back to Butte was long and exhausting but uneventful. Sadie slept as she had on the way out—and he watched her as he had done then.

He loved her now, couldn't get enough of looking at her. When she shifted in her seat and her shirttails parted to expose some pale-blue lace, he smiled. He knew all about Sadie's underwear now. It was wonderful.

But she was more wonderful. He was blessed.

"So, how'd it go?" Martha had enough discretion to wait until they'd been home overnight before turning up in Sadie's office the next morning, eyes wide and curious. "Ah, I see a ring!"

She grabbed Sadie's hand, exclaiming over her rings. "They're perfect. They're you!"

And Sadie nodded. She even managed a smile. Outwardly she could do that. It was inside she was hurting.

"You look tanned and beautiful and exhausted," Martha decided. "I hope the exhaustion is from not enough sleep." She eyed Sadie speculatively. "So, inquiring friends want to know. Did you...?" She waggled her eyebrows.

Sadie nodded, but didn't meet her gaze.

Martha peered at her more closely. "Don't tell me he's that bad in bed?" She sounded appalled.

"No!" Sadie went crimson. Couldn't help it. "He was—it was—wonderful."

"Yeah. I can tell how thrilled you are." Martha's tone was dry.

"It's just…there are…there *is*…a problem."

"Shall I kill him? Or just injure him?"

Sadie shook her head. It was so good to have a friend like Martha, who always took her side, no matter what. She smiled again. "Probably not kill him. Eddie needs his mother, and you wouldn't do him much good if they locked you up."

"Okay. Tell me what to do and I'll do it."

"I don't think there's anything you can do," Sadie said. She wondered if she dared take Martha into her confidence, then decided that she had to. Maybe Martha would think Spence was right. Maybe she was the one who was being foolish. Not him.

So she told Martha what had happened. "It was a wonderful week. A perfect week," she finished. "I love him. And I know he loves me. But we can't talk about this. He *won't* talk about it. Am I crazy? Am I wrong?"

Slowly, adamantly, Martha shook her head. "You're not wrong," she said. "He would be a wonderful father. Why does he think he wouldn't be?"

"I think because his father wasn't. His parents were…pretty dismal. He doesn't want the same for his kids."

"Oh, like that would happen." Martha rolled her eyes.

"I know that. You know that. Try convincing Spence of that."

"I can't," Martha said. "But you're not wrong. If you want this to work, you're going to have to."

Easier said than done, of course, once they were home and real life intervened. Spence was on the phone all the time. He was faxing and calling and sending messages on the computer. He flung himself back into work with a vengeance. And he never once mentioned the "no kids" issue.

Sadie almost began to think she'd dreamed it. But she only had to see him around Edward to know that she hadn't.

Martha brought her son into work often. She always had, especially when Theo was away sailing, which, as it was his job, happened regularly. Whenever Edward came, Sadie had always played with him. Tickled him. Played peek-a-boo with him and, now that he could fling a ball, played ball with him.

Edward was her pal. When Theo was home, Sadie even watched him so Martha and Theo could have an evening out now and then.

"You want Eddie some night?" Martha asked her. "Theo's not home. But I could always use some time to work. At least you'd have a natural lead-in."

Sadie remembered counseling Leonie just to talk to Richard. But when the shoe was on her own foot—and Spence was pretending that everything was fine—it didn't seem so easy. It was like the marriage elephant all over again. Only now it was the kid elephant in the room that neither of them could talk about.

"Yes, let me have Eddie," she said.

The evening with Eddie was a great success. He loved Sadie. Sadie loved him. He toddled over to Spence and grabbed him around the knees. "Da," he said.

"Not me," Spence said. But he didn't turn the little boy away. He picked him up and read him a story. Then the three of them ate macaroni and cheese for supper. They had jello cubes for dessert. Eddie even ate part of a jar of peas because Sadie convinced Spence to eat some, too.

"I'll bet Theo doesn't eat mushed peas," he complained. But he ate them. And seeing him do so, Eddie did, too.

Watching them together, Sadie dared to hope.

When Martha came and got him at ten, Eddie was asleep on their bed—next to Spence. Sadie went in to pick the little boy up and stood looking at the two of them, Eddie's small fingers wrapped around Spence's big thumb.

And he didn't want children?

How could he say that?

Martha took her sleeping son out of Sadie's arms and crossed her fingers. "Here's hoping," she said. "Good luck."

"Thanks," Sadie said. And after Martha went, she said to herself out loud, "just talk to him."

"We need to talk," she said baldly the next morning.

Maybe it wasn't the best time, but he was leaving for two weeks in a matter of hours, heading out for the Bahamas to see Dena and Tom Wilson, then going on to Naples to have a look at a project there. He was coming back via Ireland because he had a notion about buying some cottages near Cork for a retirement village. He had a lot of irons in his fire.

He didn't ignore her. He was attentive at home. He was the Spence she remembered at work. But the new elephant—the "child elephant" was always in the room. And she couldn't let him leave without talking about it.

"Talk? About what?" He was still keying in something on his handheld computer, but when she didn't speak, he finally glanced up.

Sadie took a breath. "Kids."

His features grew still. He didn't say anything for a long moment, as if waiting for her to continue. When she didn't, he said almost casually, "What about them?" and to underline his lack of interest, he went back to messing with the tiny computer.

Remembering Leonie, Sadie reached out and snatched it out of his hand. He looked at her then, astonished at her behavior. "I said I want to talk," she repeated.

His jaw set. "Talk, then."

"You can't just make a pronouncement in the middle of a marriage that you don't want kids."

"I can," he said. "I did. And don't start on me about telling you beforehand. You know it was impossible."

"Well, it's not impossible to rethink. To change your mind."

"I don't want to change my mind."

"Can't Edward change your mind?"

He frowned. "What's Edward got to do with it?"

"You loved him. You played with him. You ate peas for him. You fell asleep with him!"

"So?"

"So, why do you want to deprive children of a father like that? We'd be good parents, Spence!"

"You would."

"So would you! I know it!"

He didn't answer, just sat there, a human Mount Rushmore, except for the tension making a muscle tick in his jaw. They stared at each other, gazes dueling, grappling in silence. Finally he flicked off the computer without even looking at it, tucked it into his shirt pocket and stood up.

"I love you, Sadie," he said, his tone even, steady, flat. "And I think you love me—"

"I do love you, damn it!"

"Then try to understand that I'm not going to change my mind. My parents—"

"Oh, stop hiding behind your parents!"

His whole body jerked. "What did you say?"

"You heard me! You drag them out every time you don't let yourself do something. Yes, they left a lot to be desired. They were a couple of unhappy, sorry, miserable people. And if you give in to their influence, they win."

"They never won anything!"

"If you believe what they told you, they've won your mind," Sadie argued, knowing she was saying too much, cutting too deep, but unable to stop herself. "They own it. They own you!"

"The hell they do!" He was furious now. His face was scarlet. The veins in his neck stood out in sharp relief. "They never thought I could do anything. They always believed I was just like them!"

"And you believe it, too. I love you, Spence. And I believe you love me. The sad thing is, I don't believe you love yourself."

There was no sound in the room, in the house, in all of Montana, it seemed, after that. The world stopped. Sadie knew she had spoken the unforgivable truth. Spence's face simply closed up.

She didn't know how long they stood there—the silence beating between them—until finally Spence said, "I'll be gone two weeks. If you change your mind, I'll see you when I get back. If not, I suggest you leave and file for divorce."

"He told you to get a divorce?" Martha was apoplectic. If it were possible for a human being to carom off walls, Martha might have done it. She sat down in Sadie's office. She bounced up again. She paced. She banged doors. She hit window sashes. "What kind of idiot is he?"

"A stubborn one," Sadie said flatly. She felt dead inside. Gutted. She was alive but simply going through the motions. Had been since Spence had walked out the door yesterday afternoon.

"Maybe he'll be the one who comes to his senses, who changes his mind," Martha said when she finally settled down.

Sadie shook her head. "He won't change his mind."

Martha turned and looked at her closely. "Will you?"

"Will I what? Change my mind? I can't." Sadie knew that much. She'd lain awake all night thinking about it. "It's like when you left Theo in New York and came back to Montana even though he said he'd marry you. It was for the wrong reason. If I stayed with Spence now, it would be for the wrong reason. It would be because I didn't believe in him. And I do."

"So what are you going to do? Divorce him?" Martha went pale as she said the word.

"Maybe. We'll see. But I'm not going to live like this."

It was the longest two weeks of his life.

Spence, who ordinarily lived for the fast lane of travel, new faces and new places, was desperate to get home to his wife. Not that he'd said so. He'd only talked to her once—from the Bahamas.

It had been a stilted conversation. Polite. Distant. But he couldn't hang up without asking, "So, are you leaving me?" He was glad his voice hadn't betrayed any of his fear.

"I don't know yet," she'd said.

He'd sent text messages and e-mails and faxes after that, just like he had the first week that he'd known about their marriage, because he didn't want to argue. And he didn't want to hear what she had to say. She'd already said too damn much.

He tried not to think about it. She hadn't meant it. She'd just been angry. He was sure she missed him as much as he was missing her. And even though he'd liked what he found in Ireland, he could hardly wait to get home.

He even managed to catch an earlier flight out of Newark, via Minneapolis to Butte. Then, as it was still only three in the afternoon, he drove straight to the office to surprise her.

She wasn't there.

Grace Tredinnick was sitting at the computer, adjusting her glasses, then moving her head back and forth.

Spence skidded to a halt in the doorway. "What are you doing here?"

"Well, hello to you, sonny," Grace said, peering at him over the top of her spectacles. "Didn't expect you until morning."

"I got an early flight. Where's Sadie?" He looked around, up and down the hall, but he didn't see her.

"Sadie's gone."

"Gone home?"

Grace shook her head. "Gone away. That's why I'm here."

Spence felt as if all the blood drained right out of his head. Gone? Sadie? His stomach lurched. He felt suddenly hot and clammy, then cold as a Montana winter.

"Where?" His voice, even to his own ears, sounded like an old man's. "Where is she?"

"Texas. Austin, Texas. Took a job down there."

Texas? Who the hell did she know in Texas? Who cared who she knew? Why had she gone?

She loved him! She wasn't supposed to leave him!

"Left a letter and some stuff for you on your desk," Grace said.

But she'd barely got the words out before he had pushed past her into his office. There was an envelope on the desk, and next to it a small box.

Spence kicked the door shut, then sank down into his desk chair and picked up the envelope. She had written his name in her inimitable neat script on the front. He would know her writing anywhere.

Slowly he slit open the envelope and took out a single sheet of paper. More neat script. He felt a hard aching lump in his throat.

The letter said exactly what he didn't want to read—that she had taken him at his word, that she had gone. She had accepted a job working for Mateus Gonzales—starting up an office for him in Texas. It was all very simple. She never reproached him. She just said she was doing what he had suggested.

He opened the box. In it there were three rings—the two he'd given her on the airplane, the jade and Celtic gold that were so clearly her, and the one he thought he'd lost—his great-grandfather's heavy hand-carved ring.

He held them in his hand, rubbed his thumb over them, felt the smooth jade, the intricate filigree, the soft warmth of the pipestone. He rubbed them stroked them, turned them over and over, round and round. His throat ached, his eyes stung. His cheeks were already damp when his thumbnail caught on the edge of the inlay where the heart was broken.

It would get easier. Sadie knew that it would. Her new job was interesting. Mateus was easy to work with. He divided his time between Sao Paulo and Rio and Austin. So, frequently, like when she'd worked with Spence, she was left to do things on her own.

He never minded what she did. He was more laid-back than Spence. He worked hard, but he actually stopped to breathe now and then. He also believed in that wonderful Latin custom, the siesta, so while Sadie worked, in theory, longer hours, she was really just out of her apartment more. That was good because in the middle of the day she could get out and see parts of Austin, get used to the city, find new things to do and places to go.

It also meant she had less time to feel sorry for herself.

She knew she had done the right thing by leaving. She truly did love Spence enough to know that she couldn't live with him if it meant agreeing with his parents' definition of who he was. There was so much more inside him. So much love that he had given to her and that he could give to their children, if only he learned to spare some for himself.

He believed in himself at work. How could he not do the same at home? With her? He could. Sadie knew he could.

But it got harder and harder to stick it out on the moral high ground when days turned into weeks and weeks turned into a month and then two—and Spence never came.

She'd been sure he would. He would read her letter and understand. He would come after her and take her home again. She certainly hadn't made a secret of where she was.

She stayed in touch with Martha. She talked on the phone

with Grace. Once she'd even talked to him when he'd answered Grace's office phone.

"Sadie?" He almost choked on her name when she'd asked for Grace.

She had already done her choking when she'd heard his gruff, "Tyack Enterprises," seconds before.

"Hello, Spence," she said coolly. "How are you?"

"I'm…good. Doing fine." His cadence quickened. "Just off to Ireland again. The project there is taking off. It's going to be—" He stopped. "Never mind. I'm sure you're not interested. You've probably got a lot of equally interesting stuff going on down there."

"Quite a few things," she said airily. "Lots of excitement. We went to Rio last month. Mateus keeps me busy."

"I'm sure. Right. Here's Grace," he said abruptly, and the next thing she knew she had been handed over to the older woman.

It was the only time she'd talked to him. But it disturbed her dreams for the rest of the week. And she was only getting her equilibrium back when Mateus breezed into the office one morning and said, "Congratulate me. I'm engaged."

As he had been clearly smitten with a young *carioca* woman called Cristina when he and Sadie had been in Rio, it was not a big surprise.

"That's wonderful," Sadie said. "I'm so happy for you."

And of course she was. But it made her go home and weep for the love she'd lost. She hadn't filed for a divorce yet, but she expected any day to be served papers by Spence. There was no reason why he shouldn't. She'd left him. He could get the divorce and marry Dena now, exactly the way he'd wanted.

"Has he said anything about divorce?" she asked Martha the next time they talked. She'd told Martha about Mateus's engagement, and half expected to hear that Spence was contemplating the same.

"You think he'd tell me?" Martha said. "He doesn't talk to any of us. Not much. Oh, maybe he chats with Grace. Mostly he's gone."

Working? Sadie wondered. Or lining up a new wife?

She tormented herself with thoughts like that on a regular basis. She wished she could get past it. Get past *him*. But sometimes it felt as if she'd been born loving Spencer Tyack, and digging him out of her life—and her heart—was going to be a rest-of-her-lifetime project.

She told herself for the hundredth time this week to get started on it as she carried her week's dirty clothes down to the apartment complex laundry room. She took great pleasure in grabbing each piece of clothing and stuffing it unceremoniously into the washing machine, then adding the soap and dumping in the bleach. She needed bleach for her brain she thought. Something to get rid of Spence.

A shadow fell across her as she was putting in her quarters. "Sorry," she said without turning around, "I've taken the last one. You can have the washer after me."

"I don't want the washer. I want you."

At the sounds of that gruff, dear, familiar voice, she spun around, slinging quarters everywhere. *"Spence!"*

She wanted to run to him, grab him, hang on and never let him go. But he made no move toward her. He stood in the doorway, his thumbs hooked in his belt loops, looking like a gunfighter. His throat worked. He wet his lips, then let out a shaky breath.

"If you'll have me…and my children," he said. He didn't smile, but there was a light—a fire—in his eyes as they met hers.

"Oh, Spence!" She flew at him then, practically knocking him flat. And she knew the joy of his arms coming around her, crushing her to him, hanging on to her as if she were the only thing keeping him from drowning.

"Oh, God, Sadie, I missed you!" He said the words against her mouth, punctuated them with kisses, then buried his face into the curve of her neck, his arms still clutching her as if he'd never let her go.

That was all right with Sadie. She had lived too long for this moment, had dreamed of it too many times. And had, for a long time now been afraid it would never come.

"Excuse me?" A voice behind Spence sounded tentative. A tall black woman with beautifully beaded hair was looking bemusedly at them. "I just need to get to the dryer, please."

They stumbled apart, but Spence hung on to Sadie's hand as they stepped out of the way. "Come on," she said, "come upstairs."

Ordinarily she stayed and read a book while she did her laundry. Not today. She hauled Spence after her up the steps. The apartment was boring, nondescript, lonely. Not today.

"Why?" she asked him when she had him inside the door and their arms were around each other again. "After all these months, why now? What happened?"

"Mateus got engaged."

"What?" Sadie's jaw dropped. She couldn't believe her ears. "Mateus? What does Mateus have to do with it?"

"I…I thought you…and he…" Spence shook his head. "You left me. You went to him. He's…a catch. He probably wouldn't mind having a dozen kids." He shrugged. "I couldn't stand in your way."

Sadie was speechless. Mateus? She and Mateus? If it hadn't been so painful, it might have been funny. "No," she said at last. "We've never—"

"I didn't know. I wasn't fair to you, Sadie. I know that. And you're right. You would be a good mother."

"If we couldn't have kids, Spence, I could live without them." She already knew that. It would hurt. But she would survive. If she had him, she would always survive.

"If we don't, we can adopt some," he said.

"You changed your mind." It wasn't a question. She didn't need to ask the question. She could see the answer—the transformation—in his eyes. In the way he looked at her. In the way he smiled.

He loosed his grip on her and held up a hand for her to see. Next to the rose gold of the wedding band he still wore—the wedding band she'd given him—was the pipestone ring she'd returned.

"Grandpa changed my mind," he said. "And Richard Carstairs."

Sadie gaped. She pulled him over to her lumpy secondhand sofa and pulled him down on it, holding his hand, looking at the ring, running her finger over the inlaid heart. "It isn't broken anymore."

He shook his head. "I fixed it. Got a new piece. It's whole now." He didn't say the words, but she heard them anyway: *whole...like me.*

"The ring brought back a lot of memories. More good than bad," he said quickly. "My granddad was the one good part of my childhood. When I had it, when I started wearing it again, I started remembering him. He used to tell me not to listen to them—my parents. He used to say they tried to hurt me because they were hurting inside. He said they were sad and he wished he could do something to change who they were but he couldn't. 'They have to find it in themselves,' he said. 'It's inside you,' he used to tell me. 'You can be who you want to be.' I always thought he meant about business. I never thought beyond it. Not to my life, to the people I love. Now I realize it's about us, too."

He lifted her hand to his lips and kissed them lightly. "I got a call from Richard a few weeks ago. He and Leonie are having a baby."

Sadie didn't know whether to laugh or cry. "That's wonderful."

"It is." And he sounded like he meant it. "He said thanks, by the way. He said you woke them up, made them talk to each other, made him think about decisions he'd already made without even consulting his wife. Made him realize he'd made them because he was scared. A lot like me," Spence told her.

"I didn't want to be like my parents. Mostly I didn't want to not be the man I wanted to be, that you believed I could be. I was terrified. Still am." He smiled shakily. "But I figure Grandpa might be right, that if I work at it and take the risk, I can be the man I want to be—your husband, the father of your children, the man you love and who will love you—for the rest of our lives."

She was crying then, and hugging him, kissing him, wiping away tears that she thought were hers but might have been his. "I love you so much," she whispered, her voice breaking. "I thought I'd lost you. I thought you'd never come."

"I came as soon as I thought I had a chance. Do I?" His eyes searched hers.

"Oh, yes," Sadie answered. "Oh, my love, yes!"

It was the best Christmas Spence had ever had.

The snow was flying. The temperature was far below zero. The winds were howling out of the north, and the scene was as far as one could imagine from their Fijian honeymoon. It was a long way from Austin, too, where five months ago he had gone to bring her home.

But it was the best place in the world to be this morning, lying on the sofa with Sadie wrapped in his arms, looking at the Christmas tree—the first one they'd shared—which they had decorated together with ornaments they'd made to symbolize places they'd been, people they'd known.

Sadie had made a tiny papier-mâché house that looked like Spence's Copper King mansion. He'd carved a little birch canoe. They'd gone to Ireland and brought back a shamrock and to Cornwall and brought back a flag of St. Piran. Mateus had sent them a miniature map of Texas and, of course, one of Brazil. They had a plaster of paris circle of Edward's tiny hand, and a Statue of Liberty to recall their New York courthouse experience, and half a dozen others, including an exquisitely detailed copy of their Nanumi treehouse *bure* which Mrs. Isogawa had made for them.

"It's lovely, isn't it?" she said, snuggling close and leaning up to kiss his stubbled jaw.

"Perfect," Spence agreed. "Couldn't be better." Life couldn't be better as far as he was concerned.

"No, not quite perfect," Sadie said. "That one Grace made is out of place."

"What one?"

"There. Behind the *bure*. I can't think how it got there. Could you move it? Then it will be perfect."

"It's fine. Don't fuss." He kissed her.

"But it would be better…" She looked at him hopefully and grinned.

Sighing, he got up off the sofa and padded across the rug to the tree. "Which ornament Grace made?" Grace made a lot of god-awful ornaments. Knitted things like tiny antimacassars and dangly things that were supposed to be stars but looked more like Martian antennae.

"Behind the *bure*. See it?"

He plucked out another of Grace's knitted efforts. "This?" But when he got a closer look, he realized it wasn't an ornament. "Why does Grace knit booties for Christmas ornaments?"

"She doesn't," Sadie said, smiling. "She knits them for babies."

Spence stared. He swallowed. He looked at Sadie, dazed, disbelieving, and yet… "Is she—I mean, *are you*—sure?"

Sadie nodded, still smiling.

He felt oddly breathless. "Are you…all right?" He looked worried, nervous.

"I'm fine. Are you?" She was still smiling, but there was a hint of apprehension in her tone.

Was he? Spence thought about it. He thought about the burden, the stress, the responsibility, the potential for disaster, the sleepless nights and all the times his child would cry and he would not understand.

And then he thought about sharing a child with Sadie— about the honor and joy of being allowed to be a part of someone else's life—and a slow delighted smile spread across his face.

He crossed the room and wrapped his arms around his wife and kissed her. "Thanks to you, Sadie my love, I've never been better in my life."

Mediterranean Men

Let them sweep you off your feet!

Gorgeous Greeks

The Greek Bridegroom by Helen Bianchin
The Greek Tycoon's Mistress by Julia James
Available 20th July 2007

Seductive Spaniards

At the Spaniard's Pleasure by Jacqueline Baird
The Spaniard's Woman by Diana Hamilton
Available 17th August 2007

Irresistible Italians

The Italian's Wife by Lynne Graham
The Italian's Passionate Proposal by Sarah Morgan
Available 21st September 2007

www.millsandboon.co.uk

FREE!

4 Books
and a surprise gift!

We would like to take this opportunity to thank you for reading this Mills & Boon® book by offering you the chance to take FOUR more specially selected titles from the Modern™ series absolutely FREE! We're also making this offer to introduce you to the benefits of the Mills & Boon® Reader Service™—

- ★ **FREE home delivery**
- ★ **FREE gifts and competitions**
- ★ **FREE monthly Newsletter**
- ★ **Exclusive Reader Service offers**
- ★ **Books available before they're in the shops**

Accepting these FREE books and gift places you under no obligation to buy, you may cancel at any time, even after receiving your free shipment. Simply complete your details below and return the entire page to the address below. You don't even need a stamp!

YES! Please send me 4 free Modern books and a surprise gift. I understand that unless you hear from me, I will receive 6 superb new titles every month for just £2.89 each, postage and packing free. I am under no obligation to purchase any books and may cancel my subscription at any time. The free books and gift will be mine to keep in any case.

P7ZEF

Ms/Mrs/Miss/Mr ....Initials ....
BLOCK CAPITALS PLEASE
Surname ....
Address ....
....
....Postcode ....

Send this whole page to:
UK: FREEPOST CN81, Croydon, CR9 3WZ